Praise for *Freedom Lessons*

"This powerful story of lives shaped by school integration in the deep South shows us the fear and deeply held prejudices that marked the time, the place, and the people. But we also see the kindness, courage, and risks that offered hope and ignited change. Sanchez is a masterful storyteller. Her characters leaped off the page into my heart—where they've stayed. *Freedom Lessons* illustrates how far we've come, while reminding us how much more we have to do."

—Donna Cameron, award-winning author
of *A Year of Living Kindly*

"Sanchez offers a rare look at a tumultuous period in our nation's history—the desegregation of the schools . . . Sanchez deftly jumps between perspectives, fully immersing the reader in a different time and place. Heart-wrenching at times, *Freedom Lessons* will leave you inspired and wanting more. Sanchez gives us much to think about that is relevant even today. A captivating new voice!"

—Michelle Cox, author of the Henrietta
and Inspector Howard series

"*Freedom Lessons* is an essential read for learners of all ages, especially high school students, with accurate portrayals of the south, and characters that readers connect with instantly."

—Mia Owusu Antwi,
High School Student

"In her riveting novel, Sanchez makes us feel the pain of a Louisiana community as deeply rooted prejudice undercuts school integration . . . gives us a glimpse into the truth of a highly flawed time and place, and the corrosive nature of prejudice that unfortunately persists today."

—Michelle Cameron, author of *The Fruit of Her Hands* and *Beyond the Ghetto Gates*

"*Freedom Lessons* reminds us of a dark period in our history, and of the importance of an equal opportunity education for all. A must read for our generation and generations to come."

—Kari Bovee, author of the Annie Oakley Mystery series

"A poignant snapshot of the real-life impact of integration in the American south during a single school year in 1969, when one step forward was usually accompanied by another, often worse, step back. A reminder that genuine cultural change requires so much more than the right intentions and a good heart."

—Rita Dragonette, author of *The Fourteenth of September*

"An excellent source to teach current and future generations about The Crossover. Eileen succeeds where historians and academics like myself fail—recounting major societal events through the inescapable and complex humanity of her characters. Eileen fully delivers on the challenge of framing what teaching and learning was during this era, and *Freedom Lessons* forces us to ask the question of what it should be now."

—Michael R. Hicks, Ed.D., Assistant Professor of Education, Centenary College of Louisiana

Freedom
Lessons

Freedom Lessons

A Novel

Eileen Harrison Sanchez

She Writes Press, a BookSparks imprint
A Division of SparkPointStudio, LLC.

Published 2019

Printed in the United States of America

ISBN: 978-1-63152-610-7
ISBN: 978-1-63152-611-4
Library of Congress Control Number: 2019942982

For information, address:
She Writes Press, 1569 Solano Ave #546, Berkeley, CA 94707

She Writes Press is a division of SparkPoint Studio, LLC.All company and/or product names may be trade names, logos, trademarks, and/or registered trademarks and are the property of their respective owners.

This is a work of fiction based on personal experience and on primary sources, personal interviews, and a dissertation documenting the experiences of others during the school year of 1969–70.
Names, characters, places, and incidents either are the product of the author's imagination or are used fictitiously. Any resemblance to actual persons, living or dead, is entirely coincidental.

Names and identifying characteristics have been changed to protect the privacy of certain individuals.

I am most grateful for Gary L. Clarke's permission to use information and phrases from his dissertation, "Even the Books Were Separate: Court-Mandated Desegregation and Educators' Professional Lives During the Caddo Crossover of 1969-70."

Permission given for the use of the term or phrase "Even the books were separate", "The Crossover", "Freedom of Choice ","I'm going to graduate", "you know we need someone to discipline the Black kids", "we've been robbed", "I only want the best to keep their classes." Permission to use the background of the high school students' experiences from the narratives in the dissertation. Used examples of no black cheerleaders, no black football players on the bench, no black voices in student government, school walkouts and boycotts, and parents bringing lunch to students on the lawn during a walkout to tell the story from a student point of view.

The use of the words "Negro" and "colored", though not politically correct by today's standards, is era-specific and not intended in any kind of pejorative sense.

For my mother, Peg Harrison,
who told a good story and
encouraged me to write one.

Author Note

May 17, 1954: *Brown v. Board of Education of Topeka* was a landmark US Supreme Court case. The court unanimously declared that state laws establishing separate public schools for black and white students was unconstitutional. In 1955, the court ordered states to desegregate "with all deliberate speed."

July 2, 1964: President Lyndon B. Johnson signed the Civil Rights Act of 1964, which allowed the federal government to enforce desegregation. The Jim Crow laws of the South were abolished.

Freedom of Choice: A political practice that southern districts adopted in the 1950s and '60s to delay court-mandated desegregation. Dual zoning of housing—one for blacks, one for whites—was common in the South. Students had the "free choice" to attend a school that was not in their neighborhood. Few made that choice; most students continued to attend racially identifiable schools.

Chapter 1

❧

Colleen

Wednesday, July 2, 1969

Heat shimmered off the highway in waves that created the illusion of puddles. Colleen and Miguel passed a bank with one of those new digital clocks outside. At first, Colleen thought the flashing 106 was the time. It was the temperature.

Sweat trickled down her back. *Deal with it*, she told herself. *It's not Vietnam. He's safe and we're together.*

Once they crossed the Mississippi River, the landscape changed from cypress trees draped with Spanish moss to flowering swamp plants. Bayous threaded the low-lying sections of the river plain.

She was entertaining herself with the little rainbows rising from the puddle mirage, when she noticed a wavy mist through the windshield. She blinked. It was still there and rising from the hood of the car.

"Miguel," Colleen said, "is it really so hot that the hood is steaming?"

"Qué está pasando?" Miguel veered onto the narrow shoulder and opened the car's hood.

"Yes, what is happening?" she replied. More Spanish streamed from his direction. Colleen stepped out, pressing her fingertips to her temples.

Just three days earlier, she and Miguel had married after a six-month engagement. Impulsive as it seemed to surprised friends and family, it was a simple decision. Life was better when they were together. Since then, they'd driven 1,500 miles from New Jersey. This trip—from the place that had always meant home for Colleen to the Louisiana army base where Miguel would serve as a drill sergeant—was meant to be the start of their honeymoon.

"*Dios mío!* The bypass hose is busted. The engine overheated."

Colleen looked around. "What will we do?"

These back roads from Mississippi to West Louisiana were like nothing she'd ever seen. Highways became narrow, unlined passages with barely enough room for two lanes. They'd passed lawns strewn with rusted cars and shacks with tin roofs—not the stately mansions she'd expected.

But now there were no houses in sight, not even a shack with a wringer washing machine on the porch.

"We're so close," Miguel said. "The town line is down the road."

But they couldn't leave the car. It contained everything they owned, including some of their wedding gifts: Corningware, a blender, and a nine-inch Sony TV.

"We can wait a bit."

Colleen closed her eyes and imagined setting up their first home. The noise of a pickup truck interrupted her daydreams. Miguel waved desperately at it. A woman hanging out of the passenger window nodded at him. The longhaired driver saluted and pulled onto the shoulder. Two rifles hung on a rack across the truck's cab.

"Hi, soldier," the woman said. "Got some car trouble?"

Miguel ran a hand across his army-regulation haircut. He explained that the car had overheated.

"Well, y'all, we can drive one of you to a garage. It's on our way." The woman gave Colleen a wide grin that revealed missing teeth. "Hop in, sweetheart."

"Yes," Miguel said. "You go, Colleen. I don't want to leave you out here alone on the highway."

Colleen didn't want to go with these strangers, but she didn't want to wait along the highway either. She gave Miguel a worried look, then stepped up.

The woman moved over to make room. When she swung into the passenger seat, Colleen shuddered at the sensation of warm breath down her neck. It turned out that another man was sitting in the back. Colleen put one hand on her bare knees to keep them from knocking and rested the other on the door handle.

The woman introduced herself as Maggie and said the men were her nephews, Jack and Jake. As they drove, she peppered Colleen with questions.

"So, that's your husband?"

"Yes."

"He's good-looking for a Mexican, not as dark as most."

"He's Cuban, not Mexican."

"Darlin', they're all the same to me."

Colleen shifted closer to the door.

"How long you been married?" Maggie asked.

"Since Saturday."

"Oh, we know what you two been doing, don't we, boys?"

The men snickered. Colleen felt a flush rise from her chest to her cheeks, and she imagined leaping out of the truck and running from these people. Surely everyone down south wouldn't be this crude, right?

After a seemingly endless drive, the truck turned onto a gravel lane and headed toward a grove of trees and a sign that proclaimed BEST MECHANICS IN WEST LOUISIANA.

Maggie reached over Colleen and opened the truck's door.

"Here you go, darlin', safe and sound." She grinned. "So you can relax now." Her sarcasm dripped like the sweat down Colleen's back.

Colleen hopped out of the truck as fast as she could, right onto wobbly legs. Her heart pounded as the truck zipped away.

There weren't any other vehicles in the garage's driveway. The building was neat, maybe freshly painted. Not sure whether to be relieved or worried that no one else was around, Colleen walked to the open bay and saw legs poking out from under a truck.

"Excuse me," she called, "but I need some help."

A voice answered, "Hold on. I need to tighten this last bolt."

As Colleen waited, she examined the garage. New tires were stacked neatly in one corner, and well-organized shelves lined every wall. In the back hung an American flag and a Confederate flag. A jolt surged through her body.

In one quick motion, the mechanic pushed himself out from under the truck and stood up. BEAU was embroidered in red on the man's blue overalls. Oil stains marked the front and sides of his pants. Except for oil-crusted fingers, he was well groomed and clean-shaven, with short hair and disconcerting blue eyes. As he wiped his hands on a towel, Colleen noticed that the skin on his right forearm was patchy and discolored with a ropey scar. She wondered if he'd had some kind of accident.

"Hi, miss, I'm Beau. Where did you come from? How is it that a pretty thing like you is standing here in my garage?"

His leering eyes unsettled her. There was a tire iron by

her feet. If she had to, she would grab it. Behind Beau and his crooked smile, the Confederate flag rustled.

Miguel had warned Colleen about how different things were in the South. He hadn't been sure she should join him in Louisiana. She didn't want him to be right.

"Our car broke down about five miles back." Colleen made herself speak up and square her shoulders. "I got a ride here. My boyfriend—I mean, my husband—is waiting at the car."

"Guess you're a missus, then." Beau's eyes passed over her body anyway.

She tugged at her shorts, but there was no way they could cover her bare legs. "A hose busted, and it overheated. Can you fix it?"

"This is your lucky day, miss—I mean, missus. I just finished work on this truck. My next stop was going to be for a burger, but I can take care of you first. Do you know what hose sprang a leak?"

"The bypass hose, and the car needs coolant."

"Sounds like you know your way around cars."

Colleen nodded at the compliment. He didn't need to know that she had trouble unlatching the hood.

"Come on with me, little lady—unless you want a beer first? I've got some in a cooler in the back." He mopped his neck with a chamois cloth that hung from his belt.

"No, thanks."

"You sure? It's a hot one, and I'm mighty thirsty."

Colleen felt her heart beat in her throat. Miguel was miles away.

She searched for her no-nonsense teacher voice, the one she had used on her students last year, her first year of teaching. "Yes, I'm sure. Can we go to my car now?"

"*Your* car?"

She wondered why that seemed to surprise him.

Beau muttered, "Little lady comes in for help but can't give me the time of day." He grabbed a hose and a container of Prestone antifreeze off a shelf and walked to the tow truck.

For the second time that afternoon, Colleen pulled herself up into the cab of a pickup. At least there wasn't a rifle rack on the back of this one.

"There he is!" Colleen's relief produced an audible sigh the moment Miguel came into view. He was sitting by the car on the side of the road. As soon as she stepped down from the truck, he grabbed her by the shoulders, looked directly into her eyes, and said, *"Lo siento! Mi amor, qué pasa?"*

She pulled away from him. She couldn't believe Miguel had called her "my love" in front of this stranger. At least the puzzled looked on Beau's face told her he didn't understand Spanish.

"Nice car you have there. Whose is it?"

Miguel stood back, looking surprised at the question. "What difference does that make?" His English mixed Jersey City twang with a Spanish accent.

"Your little lady said it was hers, that's all. Mighty classy for this neck of the woods." Beau looked under the open hood and whistled. "V-8 engine, too. No wonder the hose busted in this heat."

Beau leaned back from the car, eyebrows raised. "Where y'all from, Mexico? This is a classy car, Mercury Cougar, black leather seats, Jersey plates. Is it really yours?"

The muscles in Miguel's arms and shoulders tensed up. "This is our car, and we're on the way to Fort Polk. Can you take care of it or not?"

He added something that Colleen couldn't hear, and Beau

replied, "Sure can, soldier. I'll do that, and we can both be on our way."

After Beau replaced the hose and added antifreeze to the radiator, Miguel paid him. As they watched him drive away, Colleen said, "I've got a lot to get used to here. Let's get to the trailer park and unload the car."

As Miguel opened the door for her, Colleen said, "He thought you were Mexican. Maggie, the woman in the truck, did too."

"Yup, he did. Mexicans and Negroes are the same here. This is Jim Crow country. But when I told him I'd pay in cash, he got to work fast and stopped asking questions."

Miguel grabbed Colleen's hand and squeezed. "I never should have let you go with those people. *Lo siento.* I was sorry as soon as you drove off."

As he started the car, Colleen reached into his pocket and pulled out a cigarette. She lit it with shaky hands and took a deep drag, letting the nicotine soothe her ragged edges.

The gravel road meandered past a dozen trailer homes with just enough space between them for a car or a patio. Miguel passed a cozy-looking trailer with a FOR RENT sign and continued to a much older trailer parked at the end of the road.

"Oh my God." Colleen clapped her hand to her mouth. "You've got to be kidding. It's turquoise! It has porthole windows! Does it float too?"

"Very funny," Miguel said. "It's not that bad. And everything's included."

Colleen's heart sank, but she put on a good face. She wouldn't let her new husband know that this was not the American dream her upbringing had promised.

Inside the trailer, her resolve to make the best of the

situation faded. It was like an oven with the sun beating down on the metal enclosure. She dropped the box she was carrying and sat down heavily on a nearby sofa covered in green Naugahyde.

"Even this couch is hot!" She broke into tears.

Miguel left to go into the bedroom, leaving her feeling deserted. When he returned, he immediately pulled tape and staples off the flap of a large box.

"Here, we have this huge floor fan. You cool off, and I'll keep unloading our stuff."

She sat for a while, enjoying the breeze on her face. Then, feeling guilty, she stood to help him.

"Was the trailer with the white fence for rent when you picked this?"

"The rent for that place is forty-five dollars more per month. I didn't think we could afford it."

"Why is it so much more?"

He turned to answer her with the expression of a boy admitting it was his ball that had broken the neighbors' window.

"It has air-conditioning."

Chapter 2

❦

Colleen

Monday, July 14, 1969

T wo weeks after they settled into their trailer home, Colleen got the courage to send her parents a taped message. Things weren't going as she had hoped.

"Testing, one, two, three. Hi, Dad, Mom, you know it's me. I was . . . Oops . . ."

She couldn't tell them the truth, especially her father. He was already concerned that she had wanted to quit her teaching job to marry Miguel and move away to be an army wife. And the world he had promised her was in upheaval. The assassinations of John F. Kennedy, Martin Luther King, and Robert F. Kennedy had shocked the country. Anti–Vietnam War protests and civil rights marches were fueled by anger. The North was no better than the South. He didn't have to remind her how the Newark riots had police on alert and had closed the store that Colleen worked in part-time. The future was uncertain. Her father reluctantly relented when he saw that she was resolved to live her own life.

Miguel was drafted a year out of college with a 1-A classification. His advanced training assignment in Fort Polk was
basically a guaranteed ticket to Da Nang Air Base. But the
luck of the draw placed him in drill sergeant school and gave
him eighteen months guaranteed in the United States, so they
moved up the wedding date. When the school year was over,
Colleen resigned from her teaching job. Wars influence lovers to
live for the present.

Her parents admired Miguel's grit and determination. His
family was part of the recent surge of Cuban immigrants who
had fled Cuba when Castro turned to communism. When he
was thirteen, his parents and eight siblings had left a comfortable life behind them and started over from nothing. Miguel
had exchanged his dreams of a major league baseball career for
an after-school paper route.

Colleen couldn't let her father down. Or herself.

She pressed the rewind button.

"The cassette player is really cool. Thanks for the gift. I'll
tape a message every day or two and mail it when I fill the reel.
It's hard not to have a phone. Use the number for our landlord
in an emergency. He'll take calls for us if we don't overdo it. I
thought you'd like to know about our trailer. I have to admit I
was surprised to see it. Turquoise is a color I like to wear, not
live in. We decided not to go to New Orleans for our honeymoon.
Instead, we went to Sears to buy an air conditioner. The sales-
man asked us how big our place was. 'Two bedrooms, a kitchen,
and a living room,' Miguel answered. What a joke! We should
have said that the entire space was eight feet wide and forty-six
feet long. Miguel installed the air conditioner last weekend in
the living room window. When it's on full blast, it could blow
you right out the door. More soon. Bye for now."

That was all she could reveal. She was worried about getting a teaching job. The previous year, she'd had four offers. Every town needed teachers. She'd had such confidence that it would be simple when she'd gone to the school board office the week before.

The low building was framed in painted cinder blocks and had a red tin roof, a metal door, and a small, square window. It looked like the VFW hall at home in New Jersey. Colleen spotted a large metal plaque that read KETTLE CREEK PARISH SCHOOL BOARD. She walked in.

The office was crowded with upset people attempting to make appointments. Behind the desk sat an equally distraught woman who kept repeating the same answer: "I'm sorry, but the superintendent is not available."

Colleen scrutinized the room, then sat down in a chair by the doorway next to a woman who appeared a bit more patient than the rest. A tight smile from her felt like an invitation, so Colleen asked, "Are all these people applying for teaching positions?"

The smile slipped away as the woman's mouth opened in surprise. "No, darlin', they're trying to keep their positions. The school board is in some kind of trouble with HEW, and rumors are flying. Didn't you read about it in the morning paper?"

"HEW?" Colleen asked.

"Health, Education, and Welfare, or maybe it stands for 'hate every white.'"

The woman gripped the pocketbook on her lap when two more people pushed through the doorway and bumped her chair.

"Oh my. I came here to get an application for a teaching job."

Her source shook her head. "Maybe you should come back tomorrow, or even next week, when things settle down."

Colleen took the advice and traded the office's chaos for the cushioned corner booth in the luncheonette across the street.

"Hi, darlin', you look a bit overcome. What's happening at that school board office?"

"I'm wondering the same thing. Do you have a newspaper I could buy?"

The waitress smiled as she handed Colleen a menu. "Just made a batch of my Luzianne iced tea; it'll cool you right down."

"That sounds perfect. Thank you."

"See if you want anything else while I get that tea. And yes, we have newspapers for customers. I'll bring you one."

Refreshed by the cool drink, Colleen scanned the paper. Nothing about schools or teachers in the front section. Then, on page nine, after the Little League schedule, a headline popped out: "School Board Tells of Plan for Faculty."

Her hands clenched as she read that the superintendent had presented a list of teacher assignments for approval to the school board for the fall session. The list was completed to meet the guidelines of the 1954 Supreme Court's order on school desegregation and federal enforcement of the court's 1964 order. Robert Finch, secretary of Health, Education, and Welfare (HEW), had scored a victory in the bitter struggle over school desegregation. The superintendent was not ready to make public announcements until he met with principals and teachers.

So that was the reason everyone was storming the parish board office. But the *Brown v. Board of Education* decision had happened fifteen years earlier, followed by the Civil Rights Act ten years later. And what had that teacher meant when she'd said HEW stood for "hate every white"?

Chapter 3

♥

Colleen

Tuesday, August 19, 1969

Someone rapped on the metal door of the trailer. Colleen opened it to see Mr. Murphy, their landlord and the owner of the trailer park, standing with his hat in his hand.

"Evenin', missus. You got a phone call today. Sounded important. It was the school board secretary looking for you. I came by, but you weren't home, and it's too late to call now. Come over first thing in the morning. Here's the number."

As he departed, he tipped his hat, leaving another smudge on the worn brim. Colleen smiled at him, every inch the southern gentleman she expected, despite his dungaree overalls and straw fedora. Colleen took the note and closed the door. It was so annoying not to have a phone. They had to use the pay phone on the base or depend on this awkward method. She needed a job. Miguel's salary of $230 per month was hard to stretch. She sang to the radio while she finished making dinner, as she dreamed about having enough money to move to the corner trailer with the picket fence or maybe go on their honeymoon.

◆ ◆ ◆

The next morning, Mrs. Murphy let Colleen in on the first knock. The four Murphy children giggled and let out a chorus of "Mornin', Mrs. Rodriguez."

Colleen's call to the school board secretary was brief and ended with her accepting an interview appointment that afternoon. Weeks earlier, she had returned "when things calmed down" and submitted an application. This was good news; she didn't want to work at the five-and-dime.

Inside the front door of the board office was the waiting room with the vinyl-cushioned chairs she had sat on a month before. This time, the room was empty, except for the same secretary, who greeted her with a smile.

As she ushered Colleen through the doorway to the superintendent's office, the man seated at the desk stood to greet her. Through round, wire-framed glasses, two piercing eyes examined her. "Welcome to Kettle Creek, Mrs. Rodriguez. I'm Superintendent Watson. Please, sit here."

The chair facing his desk was as uncomfortable as the one in the waiting room. She had to sit at the edge with her feet flat on the floor so that she wouldn't slide off.

"I appreciate your punctuality. With school starting next week, I'm eager to fill a few unexpected teaching positions."

Why unexpected? A few? Didn't he make a list weeks ago?

"What brings you to Kettle Creek, Mrs. Rodriguez?"

"My husband is stationed at the army base until June."

"I see. Is he an officer?"

"No, sir, he's a drill sergeant."

"So, would you be able to teach for the school year?"

Colleen smiled as she replied with a big yes, praying she didn't look as nervous as she felt.

"After examining your credentials, the best match I have for you is a second-grade position at West Hill School. I can offer you $4,750. Is that acceptable?"

Colleen agreed quickly. It was several thousand less than she had earned the previous year, but it was more than the five-and-dime would pay. With that, the superintendent stood up and escorted Colleen back down the hall. He asked the secretary to prepare the paperwork, shook Colleen's hand, and wished her a good year. The secretary handed Colleen a contract to sign, with her name, salary, and date of hire.

"Please press hard when you sign so I can give you the carbon copy for your records."

The woman put the carbon copy and a W-2 form into an envelope.

"Where is the school?" Colleen asked, as she took the papers.

"Oh, didn't he tell you? West Hill School is on Tulip Lane. Just go over the other side of the tracks after you pass through town."

As Colleen walked to her car, she realized that they hadn't asked for references and wondered if that was an oversight. But she didn't dare return. No need to remind them or take a chance that they'd change their mind. She sang along to the radio as she drove home.

Jan, another army wife and a teacher, was outside tending her garden when Colleen parked her car between their trailers. As Jan jammed a fistful of weeds into a bag, she said, "Colleen, you look happier than a tornado in this trailer park."

"I just had a job interview. It happened so fast. I start at West Hill School on Monday."

"West Hill?" Jan fixed her gaze on Colleen. "The second-grade spot?"

"Yes, how do you know?"

"That's the spot Mrs. Kirby refused to take. I told you that, right?"

"What?" Colleen heard her voice rise. "Who's Mrs. Kirby?"

"Old friend of mine. Got reassigned from the white school she taught in for forty years and told to report to the Negro school, West Hill. Of course, she called the school board office to say she couldn't accept the transfer."

"Negro school?"

"Bless your heart." Jan's smile was cold. "Yes. West Hill's a Negro school, sugar. The races are separate here. That's how everyone likes it." Jan shook her head as she bent to pull another weed. "Now they're sending white teachers to the black school." She added a bunch of reasons why Colleen shouldn't expect much from the students, the staff, or the facility at West Hill.

"Where are you from, Jan?"

"Mississippi, born and bred."

Colleen wondered what Jan thought of Miguel. This woman couldn't be the friend she'd hoped for. She was just like Maggie and Beau, from Colleen's first day in this town.

"What about the *Brown* decision?" Colleen scrambled to remember. The highest court in the land had finally said "separate but equal" wasn't good enough. Schools had to integrate. "I read that your superintendent had to follow the guidelines, and that was what caused the fuss in the office a few weeks ago."

"We follow the Freedom of Choice plan. Everyone can pick their school. It was working fine. Can't help that no colored chose to go to the white school."

Colleen drew a deep breath, thinking of news reports she'd seen about Negro children being escorted into their school by the National Guard. It had all seemed so far away until this minute. "I'm still going to take the job, Jan."

16

"Are you one of those bus-riding Yankees?" Jan's eyes narrowed. "Seems like you're fixin' to have some trouble."

Colleen shifted her purse from one shoulder to the other. "How am I causing trouble?"

"Trouble for you, I mean. No decent southern white woman would take that job. Mrs. Kirby was told to accept or retire. Forty years of service meant nothing."

"I'm not a southern woman." Colleen started to walk toward her door.

"You see what happens," Jan called out. "Then come talk to me."

Chapter 4

🍎

Colleen

Monday, August 25, 1969

One week later, on a sunny Monday morning, Colleen thought of every first day of school in her lifetime. The butterflies were the same as they'd always been—but now she was the teacher.

The dusty gravel road kicked up dirt as the car rolled toward the paved highway. Remembering Jan's warnings about the job, Colleen almost missed the turn for Tulip Lane. The school was a one-story brick building shaded by huge oak trees. She pulled into a spot in the small parking lot in front. A curved walkway invited her to the main door. Colleen entered and scanned the hallway for some directions. She spotted a sign announcing:

WELCOME BACK!

PARENTS AND VISITORS: PLEASE SEE OUR SECRETARY,

MRS. CORETTA WILSON, IN THE SCHOOL OFFICE.

A middle-aged Negro woman stood behind the counter, sorting papers into rows of mailboxes. She hummed as she worked and looked up when she noticed Colleen.

"Well! Good morning. May I help you?"

Colleen introduced herself as the new second-grade teacher and asked for the classroom keys. Mrs. Wilson chuckled and extended her hand with a huge smile.

"Aw, honey, you won't need any keys. Our night man opens all the doors before he leaves each morning. You can just go on down to the second door on the right. You should find some paperwork on your desk. Come back to me with any questions. The children won't arrive for over an hour."

Every school in New Jersey that Colleen had ever been in had interior hallways. This school was designed for the sweltering days of the region. As she walked out, she was amazed to see covered walkways that created open-air corridors around a central courtyard. Each classroom doorway was decorated with hanging planters blooming with lavender morning glories and the sweet fragrance of yellow petunias.

The size of the classroom was the next surprise. A large teacher's desk, twenty-four wooden student desks, and two long, low bookshelves filled the room. Cubbies with coat hooks and a storage closet fit comfortably opposite the bank of windows. The desks gleamed and smelled clean and fresh with the lemon scent of wax. In the back of the classroom was a smaller reading room with a half moon–shaped table. Behind it was a wall of shelves, each filled with books.

Jan had been wrong.

Colleen reached to take a book from the shelf. The binding tore away from the spine. Then she went to the desk, opened the large top drawer, and caught it before it hit the floor. Well, Jan had been partway wrong.

A breeze blew down from the hill and through the large windows. The interior walls were brick, and Colleen knew they would absorb the heat. The classroom was cooler than her car and bigger than the trailer she lived in.

As she tacked up the WELCOME TO SECOND GRADE bulletin board, she sensed someone else in the room. Colleen whirled around. In the doorway stood a woman with straight, smooth hair in a pageboy style. She had large brown eyes accented by tweezed, arched eyebrows. Her full lips were a rosy brown, and a white pearl necklace complemented her dark skin. She wore a long-sleeved jacket over a simple sheath dress. The heat didn't seem to affect this woman. "Calm, cool, and collected" was written all over her.

By comparison, Colleen felt underdressed in her sleeveless blouse, belted A-line skirt, and flat shoes. She knew her hair was frizzing in the humidity. Drops of sweat ran down her back. She prayed that her underarms would stay as dry as the deodorant ad had promised.

The elegant woman walked in without an invitation or introduction and started to speak. "So, I heard that you were just hired. You look young. How long have you been teaching?"

Colleen felt her heart quicken at the curt welcome, especially after the warm greeting from Mrs. Wilson. She swallowed the lump in her throat before speaking. "One year, back home in New Jersey."

"You must be a military wife."

"Yes, I am. Are you?"

"No. Except for four years at Southern University, I've lived here all my life. Our roots are deep. My mother, grandmother, and aunts were teachers here as well."

"My name is Colleen Rodriguez. What's yours?"

The woman gently fingered the pearls around her neck. "Evelyn. I'm Evelyn Glover. My room is next door. How long are you going to stay?"

The question seemed odd. It was the first day of school. Was this school a place people left? Colleen threw back her shoulders and stood taller.

"Why do you ask?"

"This is an army town. People get transferred all the time."

Colleen stopped holding her breath. That was all Evelyn had meant by her question.

"Until the end of the year. My husband is stationed here till then. He's a drill sergeant." A sudden involuntary image of his Smokey the Bear hat brought a smile to Colleen's face, which Evelyn's reply wiped away swiftly.

"Ah, not an officer's wife. Of course. Officers' wives teach at the white school. Mr. Peterson, our principal, asked me to look after you. He'll want to meet with you too. We'll talk more soon." With that, Evelyn turned on her heel and strode out.

Colleen pursed her lips. Why did she need looking after? She reached into her pocketbook for a tissue and blotted the sweat from the back of her neck.

Chapter 5

🍎

Frank

Saturday, September 6, 1969

The school year officially started with the first football game of the season. For ten years, West Hill High School had won the Negro League title. No wonder the bleachers were packed with students and parents.

Two minutes remained on the clock, and West Hill was down by three points. It was now or never.

Frank saw the opposing team's tight end fumble at the forty-yard line. He hurtled forward and scooped up the football. The ball bounced up, slipped from his right hand, bounced again. Frank caught it, gripped the leather, and it held. He heard the roar from the stands as the cheerleaders led the crowd in chanting his name.

"Frank, Frank, he's our man. If he can't do it, no one can!

"Go, team!"

Elbows in tight, flanked by a linebacker, he crossed the goal line for a touchdown, giving his team the first win of the new season. Lifting the ball above his head, his legs spread wide, he looked around for Dedra. He knew she'd led his chant. Each cheerleader was assigned a player, and she had his name. The team surrounded him, lifted him, and carried him off the field. His teammates put him down in front of the coach.

"Frank! Your papa would be proud!"

"Thank you, Coach."

Frank wished his father could have seen that play. He had taught Frank to grip the ball with fingers split and not on the point. Grip and hold, elbow in, forearm up. He could almost hear his father's voice: "That way, the ball can roll against your chest when you run."

With both hands on Frank's shoulders, Coach said, "You recovered that fumble like a pro. We won that game because of you. Too bad the Southern University scout wasn't here today."

"Do you know when he's coming?"

"End of October, I hope. If you keep playing like you did today, you have a long future ahead, with football leading the way. Times are changing, Frank; professional football teams are starting to integrate. You can do what I couldn't."

The locker room might have provided an escape from the throngs of spectators but not from Frank's teammates. Between punches on the shoulder and towel snapping, Frank was taking more hits than he had on the field.

"Hey, Frank," Willy said. "That cheerleader Dedra's been waiting for you to come out."

The room erupted into a high-pitched chorus of "Frankie! Oh, Frankie!"

But Frank didn't care. Dedra was student council president, smart, beautiful, and a cheerleader. He finished changing and promised to meet his teammates later to celebrate the win.

There she was, talking to her friends. Dedra still wore her

cheerleader uniform, which showed how great her legs were. She walked away from the chattering group to meet him.

"Frank Woods! Been waiting on you! Are you coming to the church hall? Reverend Wilford is letting us use it to celebrate."

"Yes, I'm coming. But I have something to do first, and then I have to stop home. I'll be there later."

Disappointment flashed across her face. "Later? But you're the reason we're celebrating, and my daddy is letting me stay out, but only till ten o'clock."

Frank didn't think the day could get any better and took a chance. "Can you walk with me? My mother won't mind if you stop in—in fact, she'd like it. She thinks you're a good influence. My sister is a freshman and wants to be a cheerleader like you."

Dedra hesitated, and he thought she was going to give him an excuse. Why would she want to walk to his house and then over to the church hall? Even if she did come, she would see the stop he had to make. No one knew what he did every day on his way home.

"Sure, I can walk with you. And I can help your sister when cheerleading tryouts come along. Sissy is her name, right? Hmm, I like that big smile of yours."

Frank could feel his grin stretch across his face as they walked off together. Dedra was easy to talk to, and before he realized it, they were at the intersection. He needed to tell her now.

"Can we turn here? I have to stop two streets over. It won't take long."

Frank led Dedra to the old horse-and-tractor barn that his father had rented years earlier. The hand-painted sign on the cinder-block wall still announced SHELTON'S AUTO REPAIR.

Dedra looked around. "Was this your dad's place?"

"Yes. I come by most days."

Located on a corner of the farm owned by Penelope Woods, Shelton's great-aunt, it was well situated. Cars and trucks passed through the intersection of the two-lane road leading into town and the main road out of town. But all that passing traffic meant that trash accumulated in unsightly clumps.

Frank picked up a dented soda can hidden in the scrub grass.

"What are you doing?" Dedra asked.

"Part of the agreement my dad had with Auntie Penelope was to keep the corner clean of trash."

"But, Frank . . ." Dedra frowned.

He knew why she was confused: his father had passed three years earlier. She didn't remember or had never known that local white businessmen hadn't liked the fact that Shelton had been the treasurer for the local NAACP. The trouble started after he opened his car and truck repair shop on nights and weekends. The black community preferred him to the local white establishment.

"Auntie was getting on in years and couldn't keep up the place. My dad promised to keep an eye on the property and do general cleanup."

"Do you still use the land?"

"No, but it was my job to check this corner on my way home each day. Sometimes I skipped it. I didn't come the day of the fire. Why should I pick up stuff folks just toss out the window?"

Frank stopped and took a deep breath. This wasn't a good idea. He could feel the emotion building behind his eyes. Dedra put her hand on his arm. He couldn't cry in front of her. He bent over to pick up some candy wrappers.

"You didn't come that day," she said, "so you come now."

She seemed to understand something that Frank had never admitted to anyone, something that haunted him. Because if he'd come that day like he'd been supposed to, maybe he could have stopped what had happened and his father would be alive.

Dedra handed him another soda can. The lump in Frank's throat loosened.

Frank walked around the house to enter through the kitchen door. He was late after walking Dedra home following the celebration at the church hall.

"Franklin Delano Woods, I hear you sneaking in. Come say good night to your mama."

He should have known she'd be up. She was hanging the last of the shirts she ironed for white ladies who expected them the next morning.

"Good night, Mama. Time for you to sleep too."

Heart pounding, Frank ran as fast as he could toward the heat. Flames shot above the trees. The fire was close to the garage. Someone rolled across the grass. Rolling, rolling to smother the fire engulfing the body. Frank pulled off his shirt, ready to swat the flames. Other people were running, shouting, "Stand back!" Someone shoved him aside. The man on the ground wore his father's blue jacket.

His knees buckled under him as he heard the burning man scream.

One of the men commanded, "No! Now, you be strong, son. Get your mama!"

But how could Frank tell his mother? He could hear her voice as if she were next to him. He saw her collapse to the floor, but he knew she was blocks away. He stood there as men placed his father in the back of a pickup truck and drove toward the infirmary on the army base.

Still in shock, Frank saw his father's shoe—black leather cracked from the heat—and bent to get it. A silver glint flashed next to the shoe. Frank picked it up: a small metal object with initials engraved on one side. He put it in his pocket and heard his mother calling his name.

His mother's cool hand stroked his cheek. "Frank, Frank! I heard you shout. Hush, now, hush. You were only dreaming."

Chapter 6

*

Colleen

Thursday, September 11, 1969

A t the end of each day, Evelyn stopped at Colleen's class-room to ask, "Still here, Mrs. Rodriguez?" And Colleen would smile and say, "Still here, Mrs. Glover."

Colleen's initial impression of a well-appointed classroom had quickly faded. One of her desk drawers didn't work properly, and the reading table was chipped. Some of the shelves under the students' chairs were broken, so those children stored their belongings on the floor. When the bell rang for dismissal, they moved their things to their chairs so the custodian could sweep and mop.

Her biggest disappointment was the reading books. The bindings were repaired, glued, or reinforced, and it was clear that the books were respected, but they were outdated hand-me-downs, bearing the imprint THIS BOOK BELONGS TO KETTLE CREEK ELEMENTARY SCHOOL, not THIS BOOK BELONGS TO WEST HILL SCHOOL.

Two weeks into the school year, Colleen sat at the reading table with her plan book and some of the readers spread out before her. Evelyn entered the room, sat down on a low student chair, and smiled—a bit strained, but it was still a smile, a sign of friendship. Colleen felt encouraged, seeing it. Could she be honest and ask for Evelyn's advice?

Colleen picked up one of the readers and opened to the page with Dick and Jane hurrying to help their mother take the clothes off the line because it had started to rain. Colleen had taught from the 1965 edition in her last school. In it, a Negro family with twin sisters Penny and Pam and their brother, Mike, were friends of Dick, Jane, and Sally.

"Evelyn," Colleen said, "this is a really old book, from 1956. Why don't we have the new edition?"

Evelyn's rare smile disappeared. "We take what we get, and this is what we get. Did you look at the inside page? All the books came from the white school. When they got the new books, we got 'new' ones too."

Colleen felt her eyes widen.

Evelyn shook her head. "Don't look so shocked. Some folks think we should be grateful that we have a Negro school at all. 'Separate but equal.' A friend of mine had to set up a new class-room in a white school this year, and she found out that they store the books in different stockrooms: colored and white. If they can't even mix the books, how do they think they can mix the students and the teachers?"

Colleen spoke carefully. "I'm just trying to understand how you relate stories and children like Dick and Jane to your students' lives with these old books."

"What do you mean?" Evelyn's mouth tightened.

"Since I don't have a teacher's guide, I've been writing comprehension questions for the class tomorrow."

"Comprehension questions?"

"Yes, like, did they ever paint a chair like Dick did? Or float paper boats in a puddle?"

"Of course they painted a chair! Probably painted all the chairs and the table, maybe whitewashed a fence too. You're going to waste time talking about floating paper boats?"

Colleen leaned back in her chair and almost tipped over.

"Let's work on the basics first, all right?" Evelyn said. "These students are in 2C because they need more help than 2A or 2B classes. Drill and practice, Colleen, then drill and practice again. Be sure that they write every day. Don't accept any careless work."

Evelyn stood so quickly that she almost knocked the chair over.

Colleen watched Hurricane Evelyn leave. Why had her simple question about reading create such a storm?

She rose, trying to shake the unsettling feeling Evelyn had left her with. Instead, she focused on the pride her students took in their classroom. She was used to children forgetting to push in their chairs or leaving their belongings on the floor of the closet. These were the neatest seven-year-olds she had ever seen.

While Colleen was packing up her things to leave, Evelyn returned to the classroom, playing nervously with her pearl necklace. "Colleen, can we talk a bit?"

"Sure," Colleen said. "I hope my question about the reading books didn't offend you."

Still lingering in the doorway, Evelyn shook her head. She cleared her throat.

"I was going to tell you this before. Mr. Peterson asked me to alert you to some events that happened last week not far from here. Some Negro teachers had to be escorted from their cars to the school building."

"My goodness, what happened?"

"They were assigned to the white school, along with a handful of Negro students. An angry mob outside the building demanded that they leave. The school had to be closed, for now, at least."

The words *angry mob* sent Colleen back to her hometown the night they closed the store she'd worked in. It was July 1967, and the Newark riots were on TV and the front pages of the papers. Police advised stores and residents in the community to stay indoors. The store was off a main highway and easily accessible to the crowd of rioters spilling over from the violence ten miles away. Colleen's town had been targeted because it was known to be a segregated white community.

"Well"—Colleen tried to sound confident—"are the children in danger? The teachers?"

"Mr. Peterson just wants you to know. You should be aware that these things are happening. White families are withdrawing their children from the integrated classes. There's some talk that they'll set up their own school."

"What does Mr. Peterson want us to do?"

"Nothing, Colleen." Evelyn's voice caught. "There's nothing for us to do, except do our jobs for these children."

Chapter 7

ȁ

Frank

Thursday, September 11, 1969

*T*hwack . . . thwack . . . thwack.

Frank heard the tennis ball slam again and again against the back of the school gym. A smile spread across his face when he saw Dedra in a short white skirt that revealed her shapely, athletic legs. She was playing an imaginary opponent as she practiced her forehand, aiming high, low, left, and right. Dedra returned each volley steadily and consistently.

Frank admired her powerful swing as much as the repetitive motions of her muscular arms. He stood at the edge of the pavement, his heart beating fast. His dream was that football would take him to college, to a better life. He knew Dedra had a dream too: to be the next Althea Gibson.

Finally, Dedra missed a return, and the ball rolled next to Frank's feet.

"Frank Woods, how long have you been standing there? Are you watching me?"

She walked toward him, the tennis racket swinging by her side. A rosy glow accented her big smile.

"Sure I was. You're really good. When are you going to play against a person? That wall can't take much more of you."

"None of the other girls are interested. There's no court, and the volleyball net is too high." Dedra shook her head. "Football practice must have ended a while ago. What are you still doing here?"

"I was with Coach."

Dedra zipped her tennis racket into its case and wiped her face with a small towel. "Well, I'd better get going."

Frank didn't want the moment to end. "Can I walk you home?"

Dedra lived a mile past his house on a small farm, and the trip would make him later than he already was, but he didn't care.

Dedra's smile faded. "No, my daddy wouldn't like that."

"He'd rather have you walk alone?"

"No, he doesn't know I stay here after the other girls leave. But he's strict about boys visiting. If he saw you without knowing about it first, it would be the last time you could come over."

Relieved that she was refusing him only because of her father's rules, Frank gathered the courage to try once more. "Can we walk as far as the road splits off?"

"Sure, and then you can tell me why you were talking to your coach."

Without asking, Frank lifted her bag full of books and tennis balls, and they headed down the road past the school.

Chapter 8

🍎

Evelyn

Thursday, September 11, 1969

Retreating behind her home's heavy oak door always made Evelyn feel safe. But not tonight. She was upset. Upset that her friend's picture was on the front page of the newspaper. Upset that she had become emotional in front of Colleen as she'd told the story. What had she been thinking?

That Colleen. How could a white teacher know how to teach these youngsters? A white woman with no history in this part of the world, who'd never been to church with her students, who didn't know their brothers, sisters, parents. Who'd be gone soon enough, most likely.

Evelyn sat heavily at her kitchen table, with its one place mat, and waited for the water to boil for tea. She'd lived alone since her parents had passed.

The newspaper was still open to the photo, just as she'd left it. Mildred's face was in the center of the picture. She looked determined and strong, her eyes fixed on the camera, and Evelyn felt a surge of admiration for her dear friend. By contrast, the Negro woman standing behind Mildred was looking down, fear creeping into the turn of her mouth.

The federal marshals who'd escorted the Negro teachers to their cars were in the picture too. Their heads and eyes were averted from the camera, as if they were embarrassed to be there. Evelyn read the article beneath the picture and raised her hand to cover her mouth. It included strong resistance in a comment credited to a middle-class white man: "No court order will ever end segregation down here. The government doesn't understand."

She had to agree with him.

Mildred had told Evelyn about being rushed to a police car and driven away from the angry crowd. The next day, the black teachers were allowed into the school but spent the day in a room under police guard. As if that would accomplish anything. As if that were any way to keep Mildred and the other Negro teachers safe.

The whistling of the kettle made Evelyn jump.

Chapter 9

●

Colleen

Thursday, September 11, 1969

A s she walked to her car, late from redoing the comprehension questions, Colleen thought about the Negro teachers Evelyn had told her about. How terrifying it must been for them to leave their school and see hostile white faces jeering and taunting as they passed.

At West Hill, the schoolyard was quiet. The birds weren't chirping. Even the sky was an ominous yellowish gray. Everyone else had left, including Lulu, who taught the 2B class. Colleen sometimes wished that friendly, easygoing Lulu were her mentor instead of Evelyn. She had an easy laugh and walked with a bounce to her step.

As Colleen drove into the trailer park, she stopped at the row of mailboxes. She and Miguel rarely got any mail, but today there was a small package from her father. Her heart ached as she realized how much she missed her parents.

Rushing to open the trailer door, she dropped her things on the sofa and opened the package to find the cassette she'd hoped for. She retrieved the player and sat down at the kitchen table to listen.

"Testing, testing, one, two, three."

Colleen chuckled. That was how she'd started her recording too.

"Sorry, I tried to record over my practicing, but I'm just messing it up. Ignore it. Okay. Colleen, this is your father. I can't wait for you to try out the cassette player and send me a tape. You can tape over this one or add on to it. Maybe you'll do it better than me. There was a photo in the *New York Times* of teachers near you being escorted out of their school. Please, you know how I worry. I don't want to read about you in the paper. Do you know about this? The article reported that school boards are under federal court orders to desegregate."

Unbelievable. He must have taped this message days earlier. He had known about the incident with the Negro teachers before she had.

It was time, Colleen decided, to talk to Jan, who seemed to know all the local gossip.

Jan opened the door on the first knock, and the scent of freshly chopped herbs filled the air.

"That smells so good," Colleen said. "I won't keep you. Sorry to interrupt."

"Yep, I had a great harvest from my garden, and I'm fixin' to can the tomatoes." Jan nodded toward her kitchen. Her trailer home was air-conditioned and nicely furnished. The round kitchen table had four chairs and didn't need to be jammed against one wall like Colleen's did.

Colleen held up a copy of *Instructor* magazine, her excuse for stopping by. "Thanks for lending me this. I thought you might want it back."

"You're welcome, darlin'. Could you put it on the counter? Don't want to get it dirty by touching it with these hands. How do you like working at West Hill?" Jan raised an eyebrow.

"It's working out fine," Colleen said, a note of pride edging into her voice. "I have to admit, I'm always surprised when I look at my hands and see that I'm the one who's different."

"I won't say I told you so. But those children need good teachers, and you seem hell-bent on being one."

Colleen wasn't sure that was a compliment, given the sour expression on Jan's face.

"I have a question for you, Jan. Did you hear about the schools in the next parish closing?"

"Sure did. Those parents don't want a Negro teaching white children."

"Do you think something like that could happen here?"

"Glory, no! Our Negroes know their place. Even with Freedom of Choice, they didn't choose to go to the white schools. But I'm sure glad I teach in a private school. Wouldn't you rather be with your own kind?"

Colleen gasped as if she had been punched. Did Jan think that because their skin was the same color, they were the "same kind"? "I like the school, and I feel welcome there." A little white lie, it was almost true—no reason to tell her about prickly Evelyn.

Colleen walked slowly back to her trailer. She had a lot to think about. It seemed that Jim Crow was more than laws; it was a way of life, a caste system with rules that Colleen didn't understand. Back in New Jersey, things weren't perfect, but integrated schools and workplaces were simply a fact, whether you liked it or not. Here, Negroes were second-class citizens in the minds of people like Jan. Even educated people. Even teachers.

I live in a trailer here, Colleen thought. *Back home, we'd be called white trash. So would you, Jan.*

Betty Crocker's *New Dinner for Two* was like a bible to Colleen. She took it from the shelf and cracked it open. It still had that new-book smell. Each section had an entire menu printed in a small rectangle. Tonight's menu was from the section labeled "Frankly Thrifty."

Texas Hash
Celery Hearts
Dill Pickles
Heavenly Salad
Pineapple Upside-Down Cake

Mealtimes had always been important in both Colleen's and Miguel's families. For Colleen's family, conversations about the daily news, politics, and schoolwork were interspersed with "Pass the potatoes, please" and spills cleaned up with paper napkins.

Dinner at Miguel's parents' home reflected the formality that cooks and maids had upheld when they'd lived in Cuba. The table was set with cloth napkins and everything needed for a three-course meal. Colleen's attempts to prepare dinners like Miguel's mother resulted in weight gain for both of them.

Since the air conditioner was humming in the background, Colleen didn't hear Miguel come home. He'd formed a habit of taking off his boots on the stoop outside so that he didn't grind sand and dirt into the linoleum flooring. He entered the trailer barefoot, moved behind Colleen, and gave her a big bear hug and a bigger kiss. The tenderness erupted in her body, but not the way it usually did. Colleen shuddered as she turned and started sobbing on his shoulder.

Through her sobs, she poured out the whole story of Evelyn telling her that she didn't know how to teach, the Negro teachers being escorted out of the school a few towns away, her father's message, and how he had seen a photo of the teachers in the newspaper.

Miguel offered to brown the beef and make the Texas hash. Then he suggested that they have rice instead of the rest of the menu.

Colleen felt the tension leave her shoulders. "No cake?"

Miguel shook his head as he started chopping onions. "No cake and no celery hearts, either."

She wiped her eyes, and they prepared the meal together. While they ate, Colleen told Miguel about an incident that had happened after lunch in her classroom.

"Remember Jarrod?"

"Is he the one who bounces in his chair?"

"Yes. I was at my desk, and three of the boys came running in."

"That's what boys do."

"But all of a sudden, Jarrod froze, with an awful look on his face."

"Why?"

"It took him a while, but then he said, 'Are you going to hit me like Miz Young did?'"

"What made him say that?" Miguel asked, cocking his head.

"My desk drawer was open, and he was staring at the black leather belt I told you about."

She hated the thick strap. It was long enough to wrap around her waist twice. At least the buckle had been removed, but the holes to fasten the belt were there as a reminder that it had served a more functional life. The leather was well worn, almost supple, but she hated to touch it. The strap was standard supply, just like the pencils, tape, and paper clips in the top drawer. It bothered Colleen that Jarrod had thought she would hit him with it.

"So, what are you going to do? Do you have to keep the strap in your desk?"

"I guess so. Evelyn told me that I should use it as part of my classroom management. But I could never hit a child. Still, I can't throw it out. It's school property."

"You have to keep order, Colleen. You need to find a way to let them know who's in charge. I'm a mean SOB to my troops because they need to survive in 'Nam when they leave here."

"They're children! This isn't a war. I'll find a better way."

After dinner, Miguel washed the dishes and Colleen used the table to grade papers. They continued to talk as they both worked.

"Miguel, do you know where the library in town is? Would you take me there on Saturday morning?"

"Sure, but you can use the one on the base."

"I want to get a library card and some applications for my students. They can't use the base library."

He had finished washing the dishes and was headed outside to shine his boots with Glo-Coat floor wax. He stopped in the doorway. "For your students? Why would you do that?"

"Remember I told you last year how I created a reading reward program that worked well? I thought I would do it again. You just told me I need other ideas."

"A reward program? That's your idea?" He winked at her.

Colleen rolled her eyes. "Yes, that's my idea. I'm not a drill sergeant. They earn a ticket for each book they read. The tickets go into a coffee can, and I pick out four tickets at the end of the month. On the next Saturday, those four students get to go with me to the library."

"*Ay, Dios mío!* How?"

"I'll pick them up and take them in our car."

"What are you doing?" Miguel turned back from the doorway and put down his boots and the bottle of Glo-Coat on a piece of newspaper. His voice grew stern. "Didn't you just tell me that you're worried about how those Negro teachers are being treated for crossing race lines?"

"This is different, and it isn't about me. They should have library cards."

Miguel stared at Colleen, worry etched into the lines of his face. "Are you sure you're doing the right thing?"

Colleen denied the thump-thump-thumping in her chest. "I'm sure," she told him.

But she wasn't.

Chapter 10

●

Colleen

Saturday, September 13, 1969

"Hi, Dad. Me again. I'm planning to go to the library today to get some better books for my students. All the libraries in Louisiana are integrated now, but not all the schools. I don't get it. More soon. I love you."

Colleen put the tape player away. Miguel was outside in the car, waiting to take her to the library.

Her mood lifted at the sight of the one-story brick building with its large, welcoming front door. Inside, she found a long counter where two librarians were working. One woman looked about Colleen's age. The other woman was older and wore her hair in a '50s-style beehive.

"Good morning. May I help you?" The younger woman's smile glinted. It was unusual to see an adult with braces.

Colleen smiled back. "I'd like to get a library card for myself and some applications for my students."

"Of course!" The young woman handed Colleen a preprinted, four-by-six-inch index card. "Here's a pen. I'll come back in a few minutes to look it over and check your identification."

43

Colleen completed the form, pulling out her military spouse ID and a gas bill with her address. The older librarian strode over and held out a hand for the paperwork. Her hair was pulled so tightly off her face that it stretched her skin taut. Colleen wondered if it gave her a headache.

"Excuse me." The woman squinted at Colleen's ID. "Is this application for you?"

"Yes. Why?"

As the librarian examined her, Colleen could almost feel her freckles buzz. She was used to people staring at her green eyes and red hair. When she was a kid, the local banker had given her a lollipop because she was cute. This didn't feel like that.

The librarian tilted her head. "But this application is for someone named . . . hmm, Rod-rye-kwiss? That's you?"

Colleen felt her Irish temper rising as she clenched her jaw and carefully pronounced her new name. "Yes, I'm Colleen Rodriguez. Is there a problem?"

"Do you have some other personal identification?"

"A driver's license. We moved here a few months ago."

The librarian held Colleen's license up to the light, as if it might be counterfeit. "But this doesn't say Rod-rye-kwiss."

"Right. I haven't gotten a chance to change my name yet. We just got married. I'll take care of it when we go home to New Jersey."

"Darlin', I never saw anyone that looked like you with a Mexican name." The woman shook her beehived head. "Just a moment, please. Wait here."

Colleen's face grew hot. So this was how it felt to be an outsider.

The librarian reappeared after a minute. "My boss approved your paperwork," she said with a tight smile.

Colleen reached out to take the card. The librarian seemed reluctant to let it go.

"Thank you." Colleen willed herself to stand taller, with her head high and her shoulders back. "I also need some applications for my students."

"You're a teacher? Why didn't you tell me so before?"

Tension rose up Colleen's back. She nodded toward the younger librarian. "I did ask for student applications from the woman over there."

"Where do you teach?"

"West Hill School."

The librarian stepped back from the counter. "West Hill School? On Tulip Lane? That's the black school."

Colleen gritted her teeth. *Is there a* WHITES ONLY *sign I missed somewhere?*

"Yes, that's right. I need twenty-four applications." Colleen splayed her fingers on the counter to stop her hands from trembling.

"I don't have that many here at the counter. You'll have to wait."

The librarian walked into the back office. Finally, Mrs. Beehive returned with a stack of cards.

"Can you explain why you're doing this and not the parents of your students?" She pursed her lips, as if impersonating the librarians who'd shushed Colleen and her giggling friends back in the high school library.

"Where I taught in New Jersey, every student received a library card at the end of first grade. The teachers handed them out. My students are in second grade, and none of them have a card."

"That's not our policy. We have to have parental permission

for each of these cards. And if any books are not returned, there will be a fine, or even full payment, for the book. Do you understand that?"

Colleen struggled with her rising anger but responded politely. "Of course. The children will be with me when they take out books, and I will help to return them."

"But West Hill is across town. Are you bringing them all here on a school-day field trip? We would have to make arrangements for such a large group."

"Only a few at a time, on Saturdays, as soon as they get their cards."

The librarian slapped the pile of application cards on the counter. She gave Colleen an amused look. "Well, Mrs. Rodrye-kwiss, bless your heart. You are just what we need in this library. You come back to me with those permission slips."

Colleen picked up the stack of applications and walked out of the library.

Rodriguez, Rodriguez.

As she left the building, she felt a set of piercing eyes follow her, and a chill traveled down her spine.

Chapter 11

🍎

Colleen

Tuesday, September 16, 1969

C olleen sat at the large table in her classroom, eating her lunch alone and grading papers, when a child's cry interrupted her contemplative mood. Cynthia ran in from recess with tears in her eyes and four barrettes clutched in her hand. Her dress was crumbled and dirty. One knee was scraped raw.

Colleen rose so quickly that she knocked over her chair.

"Cynthia, what happened? Come and sit over here with me."

Tears cleaned the red dirt from her cheeks as Cynthia sobbed and shuddered, trying to catch her breath to answer.

"Miz Rodriguez, I was racing with the boys. I was winning! But someone tripped me! Is my dress ruined? My mama will be mad."

"Let me wipe your face, Cynthia. Come to the sink. We can fix this together."

Colleen dampened a napkin from her lunch bag to clean the dusty red dirt off the child's face. Then she gently washed Cynthia's brown knee. It might need a Band-Aid, but that could wait. Colleen saw that the four barrettes belonged to four unraveled braids. The girls called them plaits. But it didn't matter what they were called, Colleen had never braided a Negro girl's hair before.

"Cynthia, can I dust off your dress? Should I fix your hair?"

Cynthia slowly calmed down as she let Colleen clean her up, her sobs growing softer. Cynthia's hair was soft, and the tight curls stretched into long, wavy sections that sprang back as Colleen tried to braid them. When she struggled to fasten the barrettes to Cynthia's hair, the little girl stared at Colleen's arms.

Finally, she looked up. "Miz Rodriguez, why do you have so many pimples on your arms?"

"Pimples?" Colleen frowned down at her arms and then laughed. "Oh, you mean freckles. I get them from the sun."

"The sun? How does the sun give them to you? Will I get some? I done never heard 'bout that."

Just as Colleen finished the last braid, her class arrived at the door with Lulu, who had playground duty that day. Colleen looked up to see Lulu's expression shift from a puzzled look to a wide grin.

"Good afternoon, Mrs. Rodriguez. I have your children here. Are you ready for them?"

"Yes, thank you, Mrs. Moberly."

As Colleen guided Cynthia to her seat, she realized that her lunch and the students' papers were all over the table she needed for the lesson she had planned. If she didn't clean it up quickly, Jarrod would be up to his "funtics." Jarrod was a large boy with closely cropped black curls. His ears stood away from his face, and when he looked at someone, it was often through squinted eyes. Maybe she should refer him to the school nurse for a vision screening.

"Jarrod, could you take this book to Mrs. Moberly?" She

quickly chose a volume from the bookcase. Lulu would understand since they had an agreement to send their wiggliest students on errands to each other when necessary.

Now what?

She scanned the class and realized she could count on Linkston, her little professor, with his tortoiseshell-frame glasses. Typically dressed in pressed pants and a sweater vest over a white shirt, he was always the first one at school. She asked him to pass out the papers and scurried around the back of the room, collecting and organizing things so she would be ready by the time Jarrod returned.

At the end of the day, once the students had gone home, Colleen knocked on the door to Lulu's classroom.

"Can I ask your advice on something?" Colleen said. "I went to the town library, and . . ." Her voice trailed off.

Lulu's face was grave as she looked up from her desk. "Let me guess. Did ole Miz Meriwether give you a problem, the one with her hair slicked tight around her head?"

Colleen sank into one of the low student chairs. "First she couldn't pronounce Rodriguez, and then she didn't want to give me library card applications for the class."

"For your class? Why would you want those?"

Colleen explained her plan. Lulu pinched off spent flowers from her plants on the window shelf as she listened. "How will the children get to the library?" she asked.

Colleen remembered Miguel's concern. "I can take them in my car."

The worried expression on Lulu's face didn't surprise Colleen. "Really? Have you told the parents?"

"Not yet. That's why I wanted to talk to you. What do you think?"

Lulu tossed the pruned petals into the trash. "Maybe it

would work for me because this is where I've always lived. We all do extra things for the children. Families don't expect it, but the teachers at West Hill are like second parents. Everyone looks out for everyone. But I don't know about the library and those women, or if the parents will agree to your driving their children around."

Lulu went to the sink and filled a bottle to water the hanging plants by the doorway.

Colleen crossed her arms. "I did this at my last school."

"You know it's not the same." Lulu shook her head. "The rest of us go to the same church and have been in the students' homes. Some of the parents were my schoolmates."

Colleen watched Lulu pack her schoolbag and tidy her desk. She thought about how she had never been in a Negro's home.

"This is important to me." Colleen stepped toward Lulu. "Will you help me get the parents' permission?"

Lulu sighed. "Oh, Lordy. Let me start with Rachel's mother, Annie Mae Woods. If she agrees, I can talk to a few at church this Sunday. I'll explain and see what they say."

"Oh, Lulu, that would be wonderful." It was all Colleen could do not to hug her. "Do you think I should come and meet with the parents too?"

Lulu closed her eyes and took a deep breath. "One thing at a time, Colleen. One thing at a time."

"Mrs. Rodriguez?" Mr. Peterson called, as Colleen passed his office. "Do you have some time to speak with me before you leave today?"

A tall, broad-shouldered man, Mr. Peterson carried himself like the Marine lieutenant he'd been during the Korean War. His Afro hairstyle set him apart from other men of his generation and helped him connect with the youth he now served. He greeted each student, parent, and teacher by name and always remembered the last conversation he'd had with that person. Colleen wished she could tell him about how she felt having Evelyn as her mentor. Talking to Lulu was so much easier.

He came around the partition to invite her into his office. Despite the heat of the day, he was formally dressed in a suit with a shirt and tie. Colleen sat in a chair facing his organized desk. She remembered how her desk pad was stuffed with notes under the sides and stacks of paper-clipped things to do. The only papers on Mr. Peterson's desk were neatly arranged in the in/out double-tiered letter tray.

"You've stayed here late again, Mrs. Rodriguez. Were you meeting with Miss Glover today?"

Colleen thought she would be comfortable speaking with him, but as she twisted her wedding band, she noticed that her palms were damp.

"No, actually, I was speaking with Mrs. Moberly. I wanted her opinion on something I'm planning with my class."

"I'm pleased to know that you're seeking advice from other teachers, in addition to Miss Glover. We have good teachers here, and every one of them can be helpful to you."

Colleen sighed and took in a deep breath.

"Are you feeling well, Mrs. Rodriguez?"

"Oh, yes, sir. I'm just glad to hear that. I find Mrs. Moberly easy to talk to."

Mr. Peterson sat back in his chair and laughed. "Is that another way of saying that Miss Glover isn't easy to talk to?"

Colleen felt a blush creeping up her neck and into her cheeks, but Mr. Peterson's smile didn't falter. "Let me tell you a story, Mrs. Rodriguez. It's about a young Negro woman who loved to read and a white woman named Rosa Keller. In 1953,

Mrs. Keller was the first woman appointed to the New Orleans library board."

Colleen shifted so that she could cross her ankles.

"Mrs. Keller was surprised that the library was segregated," Mr. Peterson continued. "She was from New York. Isn't that where you're from, Mrs. Rodriguez?"

"No, sir, I'm from New Jersey."

"I see. Well, Mrs. Keller suggested that the State Library of Louisiana in New Orleans be open to everyone, especially schoolchildren."

"I have to agree with that. I was just talking to Mrs. Moberly about the town library."

"Were you, now? What a coincidence."

Sure is, Colleen thought. Had Lulu told Mr. Peterson about their conversation? He flicked an invisible speck of dirt from his desk. "Our town library has been integrated since 1958. Strange, isn't it? Libraries are integrated, but the bathrooms and the schools aren't. We can thank Mrs. Keller, who had the courage to speak up."

"So, if I wanted to, I could take my students to the library?"

He raised his right hand. Colleen remembered what Lulu had said: *One thing at a time.*

"Listen to the rest of the story, Mrs. Rodriguez. Some time ago, our community was chosen to have a branch of the state library. Since it was to be built with federal funds, it would be integrated like the main branch in New Orleans. The young Negro woman I mentioned earlier was studying to be a teacher. She intended to be the best teacher in her family—a family I happen to know quite well. An integrated library gave her hope that she could get better books for herself and her students. Let's call her Evie."

"Evelyn?"

"Yes. Now, all summer Evie watched the workmen build that library, brick by brick. On opening day, she was up at dawn. She stood across the street, waiting for the doors to open. But something happened that day that made it so she couldn't use the library. In fact, to my knowledge, she has never gone inside that building. Maybe someday she'll tell you why."

He stood up and walked Colleen to the door. "Mrs. Rodriguez, you have a lot to learn about our community, and Miss Glover can help you. Perhaps she can learn from you too. Just think about that. But now, I believe it's time for both of us to go home and have our dinner."

Chapter 12

♥

Colleen

Monday, September 22, 1969

The morning routine of Class 2C's school day now included Book Count. Colleen looked at the tally and noticed Cynthia's column creeping up on the bar graph.

Cynthia saw it too. "Miz Rodriguez! Look, my boxes are almost as high as Rachel's! But not as high as Linkston's. I want to win!"

Colleen remembered how Cynthia had fallen while racing the boys. She smiled, thinking about how winning was important to Cynthia.

During her weekly meetings with Evelyn, her mentor's cool manner constantly punctured Colleen's newfound self-assurance. The first library trip was planned for the coming Saturday. Colleen decided that she should ask for Evelyn's advice about it at their meeting. It would break the tension one way or the other.

At the end of the school day, Colleen went to her mentor's room, as planned. Evelyn sat at a student desk, her petite frame almost the right size for the chair. She was perched with her elbows on her knees, though, her shoulders tilting forward. Her head was turned away, staring out the window.

"Is something wrong? Evelyn?" Colleen stepped forward. "Evelyn?"

"I hear you." Evelyn stood up, her face resuming its usual composed expression. "I just didn't want to answer. My friend has probably lost her job."

"Your friend? The one who the police escorted from school? Oh, I'm sorry." Colleen stood by the table where she and Evelyn usually sat, tracing a crack in its surface with her fingers.

An awkward silence stretched between the two women. Finally, Evelyn spoke. "Mr. Peterson told me you had a question about using the library."

Anxiety bubbled in Colleen's stomach. How much had Mr. Peterson told Evelyn already?

"I've been meaning to ask you for some advice. I have a reading incentive plan in my room. The children are earning points for a chance to go to the library with me on Saturdays."

"What library?" Evelyn sat at the table and shuffled some papers. "The one on the army base?"

"No, the one in town."

Evelyn's expression hardened. "Why?"

Still standing, Colleen explained her plan. "When I found out that none of my students have a library card, I decided I would help to get them. And I'll take four at a time in my car on Saturdays since there isn't money for a school bus trip."

Colleen touched the top of the chair, ready to pull it out and sit. But Evelyn seemed so lost in thought, so distracted, that Colleen didn't think she had even heard her.

"Evelyn?"

Evelyn raised her voice. "So, what *is* your question, Colleen? What do you want from me?"

Colleen didn't see any way to change the subject, so she plowed through. "When I went to the library a few weeks ago, the librarian wasn't exactly cooperative. It took a bit of time to get enough library card applications for my class."

"And?"

Colleen sat down. "It was when she found out what school I worked in that she became less cooperative."

A flash of anguish passed over Evelyn's face. "I still don't know what your question is, Colleen."

"What should I do?"

Evelyn leaned back and turned her head toward the clock. "I really can't advise you on that. What I would do about the library has nothing to do with what you can or should do."

The unspoken words hung between them: *because you're white*.

Evelyn flipped open a folder. "We still have *our* jobs. Let's try to keep them."

Chapter 13

🍎

Colleen

Tuesday, November 4, 1969

olleen stood under a tree on the grassy rise behind the school that was used for recess. It was her week for playground duty, and she was the only white person in the yard. Moments like this reminded her that she was the one who was different, who needed acceptance.

For the past four months, Colleen had lived in two different worlds. She and Miguel lived in a whites-only trailer park, even though there wasn't a sign. They went dancing on weekends at the integrated NCO club, but that didn't generate any new friendships.

Two months earlier, her students' parents had agreed to sign permission slips for library visits and cards. Mrs. Annie Mae Woods was instrumental in helping with that. Adults' cautious nods countered the gleeful greetings from children at her Saturday morning pickups. She always drove away carefully so that the tires of her car wouldn't kick up the gravel of the unpaved roads. She wanted to build these families' trust.

Colleen had grown up in an all-white community, gone to

all-white schools, and attended Mass at an all-white church. Until college, the only Negro she had ever known was Beulah, the woman her parents had employed for a few years when her mother was sick. She had had a black baby doll, if that counted for anything. When her family had moved, Beulah had stopped working for them. The doll had been a present from her mother, who knew how much Colleen missed Beulah after she left.

"Beulah!" she said aloud. Cynthia ran to her. "Miz Rodriguez, who y'all want?" Cynthia's delicate features contrasted with her tomboy ways. Today, her fine, curly hair was plaited in the usual braids, with yellow, blue, green, and red barrettes clipped to the ends of each one. So far, none had unraveled.

Colleen covered the gasp that escaped from her mouth. "Sorry, I was thinking of an old friend. Guess I said her name."

Jarrod ran by, shouting, "You cain't catch me!" and Cynthia was gone.

As the children raced away, Beulah was still on her mind and Colleen remembered an incident on a bus when she was twelve. When a weary Negro woman struggled down the aisle at the end of her workday, there were no seats left. Everyone looked away, either out the windows or into a newspaper. Colleen noticed that one of the bags the woman was carrying had cleaning supplies in it, and she remembered Beulah, so she stood up and gave the woman her seat. Heads turned, eyes blamed, and stern, silent faces denounced Colleen's offer. She lost her balance and reached for the strap above her head so that she wouldn't fall as the bus turned the corner. Her father's words came back to her: *Colleen, always treat people the way you would want to be treated. It was right of you to give up your seat.*

The recess bell rang, and the children lined up along the brick wall of the school. Colleen led them past the row of crepe myrtle trees and the trellis of morning glory vines near her classroom's door. She thought she should get a trellis for her trailer home. She felt a grin spread across her face at the idea of lavender flowers against a turquoise metal background.

Colleen held the classroom door open for the children, but they halted suddenly, and Linkston shot her a concerned look. Three white men stood inside the classroom with Mr. Peterson. Each one held a clipboard. Their dark suits, white shirts, and narrow ties set off their serious, unsmiling presence.

"Good afternoon, Mrs. Rodriguez." Mr. Peterson nodded at her. "Please go about your usual routine. We won't be in your way."

The children filed to their seats in silence, even Jarrod. Linkston, the self-appointed enforcer, didn't have to remind anyone of the rules. He looked at Colleen pleadingly and whispered, "Who are they?"

Colleen wondered the same thing, but she couldn't show her concern. Were they here to observe her because she was new? They'd never taken her references. Could something be wrong? She recognized the superintendent who had hired her.

Standing at the front of the classroom, she said, "Children, I need the Red Robins to meet me at the reading table. The rest of you can finish your math and writing practice. Is everyone ready to work?"

Wide-eyed children glanced at the white men and silently started writing. Colleen walked to the back wall and sat at the reading table so she could see the rows of students. The suits jotted something on their clipboards. Linkston sat next to her, his glasses magnifying the fear in his eyes.

Suddenly, she thought of the Negro teachers who'd been escorted out of the white school and the hostile parents shouting threats at them. Even in her serene little classroom, the presence of these white men sent a charge through the air.

As she reached over to pick up a stack of vocabulary cards, her hand trembled. Usually the children were excited to read the cards aloud, but this time, no one spoke.

"Hmm." Colleen forced an encouraging smile. "Let's see who knows this word."

Her little professor Linkston finally answered. She rewarded him by letting him hold the card. Slowly, each child read so they could hold a card.

The lesson took half the time she had planned since everyone was so timid about speaking up. The students who were completing seat work put their papers away when they were finished and sat quietly with their hands folded. Under any other circumstances, Colleen would have laughed aloud at this uncharacteristically angelic behavior.

Colleen glanced at the men, who were still furrowing their brows and scribbling on their clipboards. Would they think the children were well behaved or that she didn't give them enough to do?

"Good work, children." She felt a pulse below her eye. "I see that everyone is finished. Do you remember that today is Science Experiment Day?"

This announcement usually brought gleeful cheers. But the students sat in silence, and none of them scrambled to help her as they normally would have. While she rummaged in the side closet for her science materials, she heard whispers from the children. She swiveled to see whether the men were still taking notes.

The suits were gone as mysteriously as they had appeared.

Jarrod spoke first, still a bit hesitant. His hand went up, "Miz Rodriguez! Was that your husband?"

Cynthia shot him a quick retort. "Jarrod, her husband is an army man!"

"Are they principals like Mr. Peterson?" asked Linkston.

"Maybe, but we have work to do," Colleen answered. "Okay, where are my scientists?"

Hands shot up, and the children's faces broke into relieved smiles.

Just then, the intercom crackled. "Good afternoon, teachers and students, pardon the interruption. Teachers, please stop in the auditorium after dismissal today for a brief meeting."

Mr. Peterson rarely used the intercom system, always preferring to come personally into each classroom to make announcements. His voice sounded strained to Colleen, but it could just be that she wasn't used to hearing it broadcast from the box on the wall.

After the children left, Evelyn came to Colleen's room. Her face was stern as she rested her hands on her hips.

"Mrs. Rodriguez, he wants us now."

Colleen finished rinsing the bottle she had used for the science lesson volcano experiment. "I'm just finishing up here. Do you know what the meeting is about?"

"No, but it must have something to do with the visits we all got from the superintendent and the parish board president."

Realization dawned on Colleen. So, it hadn't been a new-teacher observation after all.

In the auditorium, the teachers sat in small groups, chattering and speculating about the unexpected meeting.

The three visitors and Mr. Peterson strode to the front of the room, and their unsmiling presence had the same effect on the teachers as it had on Colleen's class. Silence filled the space.

Colleen noticed that everyone was at the meeting: the secretaries, the custodians, and the cafeteria workers. She turned to look at Evelyn. Every muscle in her body looked tense as she sat ramrod straight, lips in a straight line. Lulu kept wiping her hands on her skirt.

A microphone had been set up, but Mr. Peterson didn't need it. His strong voice projected to the back of the auditorium. He welcomed the staff and introduced the superintendent, Mr. James Watson; the president of the parish school board, Mr. Ralph Morrow; and the principal of Kettle Creek schools, Mr. Cornelius Palmer.

"Teachers and staff, as I announced, this meeting will be brief. Mr. Watson will speak to you, and then I will have a follow-up request."

Mr. Watson seemed shorter and older than Colleen remembered, but his voice boomed through the microphone, ensuring that not a word was missed.

"Good afternoon. Last Friday, I met with officials from the Department of Health, Education, and Welfare, who informed me, 'Under explicit holdings of this court, the obligation of every school district is to terminate dual school systems at once and to operate, now and hereafter, only unitary schools.' That means that the Freedom of Choice plan we have been operating under is no longer legal. We must close the doors of our Negro schools immediately."

He paused and raised his hand to silence the gasps that escaped from the crowd.

"Starting tomorrow morning, all students, faculty, administrators, secretaries, cooks, and custodians from West Hill schools will be absorbed into the Kettle Creek schools. This involuntary transfer will take place tomorrow, without loss of school time and without loss of any positions."

Unable to contain their shock at this news, the staff let out cries of concern.

"Tomorrow?"

"The new wing just opened this year!"

"You can't close this school!"

Mr. Peterson stepped back, as if to distance himself from the superintendent and the sudden decision.

Mr. Watson didn't respond to the outcry. Once the group settled down, he continued, "All students and staff from West Hill Elementary will report to Kettle Creek Elementary. The students will be transported by bus. I will release you now, and I ask you not to share this information with parents. Leave that task to us."

Watson handed the squealing microphone to Mr. Peterson, who turned it off."Teachers and staff, I realize this is a shock." Mr. Peterson spoke slowly, his eyes moving to catch the gaze of each person present. "Do not report here tomorrow. The school is closed. Right now, I would like to see each of the teachers for kindergarten through grade five. Teachers, go to your classrooms to collect your personal belongings. All other materials, including your desks and the student desks, will be moved if necessary. Please meet Mr. Palmer and me in the Kettle Creek Elementary cafeteria at eight o'clock tomorrow morning. At that time, we will have further information regarding your assignments. The rest of the staff can please take this time to collect personal belongings and go home to your families. Tomorrow will be a long day."

Mr. Peterson walked away immediately and headed toward his office. The other men left through the side door to the parking lot. The rows of teachers started buzzing. Colleen saw tears on more than one teacher's face.

Colleen's mind raced. School closed? Transfer? Where? When she finally collected herself and looked around, Evelyn was gone.

"Lulu, where's Evelyn?"

"She's gone, said she doesn't care. Gone to tell the families in her neighborhood. Gone to spread the word."

How could they all just move into another school? Colleen would have to start over. She smoothed her dress with a shaking hand. She'd just begun to feel as if she belonged here.

She walked to the office to find out what Mr. Peterson wanted.

Mrs. Wilson stood behind the counter that separated the office from the entrance. Somehow, she managed to make the corners of her mouth turn up. "Mr. Peterson can see you next. Are you the one who asked me for keys on your first day?"

Colleen forced a smile at the memory. "I am."

"Well, honey"—Mrs. Wilson shook her head—"you just might get those keys at the next place."

One of the third-grade teachers sidled past, her head lowered.

"Mrs. Rodriguez," Mr. Peterson called from his doorway. "You may come in now."

He gestured to the same chair she'd used when he'd confided the story about Evelyn. There were deep creases in his forehead that she had never noticed before.

"Well, Mrs. Rodriguez, this will be the last time we can sit here and talk." He leaned back in his chair and took a deep breath. "You'll be pleased to know that you will be keeping the twenty-four students who are in your class."

Colleen shifted in her chair, waiting for the *but* she could see on his face. It came right away.

"Some of the classes needed to be shared," Mr. Peterson continued. "You will have an additional six students from another second-grade class."

"Six more?"

"Each class will have thirty. There aren't enough classrooms."

The weight of this information caused Colleen to slump into her chair.

"I'll have a classroom?"

"Yes, but not in the main building. Four temporary por-
tables have been moved to the backfield. You will have one of
those. Your furniture, books, and materials will be moved there
by morning."

He stood up to escort her out of the office. "I'm sure you have
many questions, but that's all the time I have right now. You're
a fine teacher, Mrs. Rodriguez." His face tightened. "You're not
one of the teachers who have to worry."

Is that because I'm white? Tears built behind Colleen's eyes,
and her temples throbbed.

Colleen paced from one end of the trailer to the other, checking
the clock in the bedroom and then in the kitchen. Miguel would
be home in an hour. Her heart raced.

Finally, she broke down and opened his carton of Marlboros.
Her hands shook, and it took her several tries to light a cigarette with a flimsy cardboard match.

By the time Miguel walked in, she had chain-smoked half
the pack. The story poured out of her, from the shock of seeing four men inside her classroom to the announcement of the
school closure.

Miguel tried to get her to focus on the positive. "You have
your class."

"And more. How am I supposed to manage thirty students?"

She reached for another cigarette. He moved the pack out of
her reach.

"The classroom is air-conditioned," he tried.

"It's a trailer with no windows!"

"Colleen, I don't know what else to say." Sadness clouded
his features, but he opened his arms, inviting her in.

Chapter 14

❖

Frank

Wednesday, November 5, 1969

"Frank, Frank! You need to wake up! Time to go! I need you to take your sisters to school. Now!"

As he got out of bed, Frank saw the worry in his mother's eyes. The previous night, her friend Evelyn had called to tell them about the closing of the black schools. There were rumors of protests from the white and black communities. Frank didn't tell his mother that he'd known already. The black coaches had told the football team. He was supposed to meet the team at the back of the school. How could he take his sisters and get there on time?

By the time he got to the kitchen, Sissy was waiting by the back door. She complained, "Mama, I don't want to go to the white school. I'm scared. Miz Glover says that the white folks don't want any of us to go to their school."

"Child, don't you worry none about those folks. And don't say things to upset your little sister, Rachel. Your brother will be by your side until you get to school."

Frank's mother hurried to finish plaiting Rachel's hair. As

she handed them their bagged lunches, she said, "Frank, you take care of your little sister. Sissy will be fine as soon as she finds her friends. I'm glad I can always count on you."

Walking down the street, Frank held Rachel's hand, but she kept pulling away. He had a hard time holding on to her. Was she going to run back home? She stopped struggling when they got to the corner and saw the usual gang of kids waiting for the bus, as they did each school morning. Frank wondered how many of them knew. Some of the boys were playing kick the can, like they always did. The group of older girls looked bored, or was it worried? Sissy, who'd fallen behind, finally caught up.

The bus driver seemed tense and limited his usual greeting to "Hurry on, y'all." Frank pushed Rachel along and found a seat for the three of them to share. The bus turned in the direction opposite their school.

"Driver! You missed the turn!"

"Wait, we're going the wrong way!"

The leader of the kick-the-can group ran up the aisle to tell the driver, who was doing his best to ignore the shouts. A girl stood up and said to the busload of students, "Don't y'all know our school closed?"

"Why?"

"Where do we go?"

"What teacher will I have?"

The bus pulled over to the side, and the driver stood up. His shoulders drooped as he delivered the message. He was a kind man, and the students listened to him.

"Sit down, now. Y'all going to the white school. It'll be a'right."

"But they hate us!" came a cry from the back.

"Your teachers will meet you there," he said.

The rest of the ride was quiet, sprinkled with hushed

67

whispers from the older students, who leaned over seats to pat a shoulder or hold a hand.

The bus stopped in front of a long, low building, and Frank watched each student hesitate as they got off. They had to walk past a lot of white folks standing along the walkway. Frank stepped into the street to get by. A few had signs that read FREE-DOM OF CHOICE, and they pushed and shoved the students who tried to move around them.

He passed Mrs. Olsen, one of the white women his mama ironed for. She didn't have a sign, but she was talking to the people who did.

"Sissy, hurry," Frank said. "You go on to the high school. Find your friends, and I'll see you later."

As they turned the corner, Rachel's teacher waved at them and smiled. "Good morning, Rachel. Is this your brother?" she asked.

It was rare that his sister didn't answer for herself. He realized how scared she must be.

He answered, "Yes, ma'am. I'm Frank."

"You can meet us here at dismissal, Frank. I hope you have a good day."

He touched his sister on the shoulder and felt her shaking. The teacher took Rachel's hand and said, "Come here, sweetie. Stand with me."

Chapter 15

🍎

Colleen

Wednesday, November 5, 1969

After she dropped Miguel off, Colleen drove toward the elementary school, the dry dirt road kicking up dust. The weather was still warm. How would they survive all day in a metal box? No classroom with huge windows to open. No redbrick walls that cooled the room naturally.

The entrance to the school was blocked. A police officer directed her around a barricade to the parking lot beside the high school. When she parked, Colleen saw crowds of people dividing the street. *Look at all those parents on the sidewalk. What do the signs say?* FREEDOM OF CHOICE? *Sure. Who exactly has a choice?*

Colleen missed Mrs. Wilson's cheerful morning greeting as she passed the main office in her new school. She knew to meet in the cafeteria, but where was it? Colleen followed a line of black teachers as they walked past a few white teachers who stood in their classroom doorways, as if on guard.

An announcement came over the loudspeaker: "All staff need to report to the cafeteria for the meeting." The group of white teachers didn't move. They glared at the parade of displaced teachers. She heard one complain, "Where are all these people going to fit?" Another said, "They don't pay me enough for this."

In the cafeteria, the black teachers stood silently in the back while the white teachers sat at the tables. No one invited anyone to sit, so Colleen stood with her colleagues from West Hill. After a compressed, to-the-point "Welcome, we have a busy day," Mr. Palmer briefed the audience. "New staff will be escorted to your classrooms. Room assignments, class lists, and school maps will be distributed now. Except for the four teachers in the trailer classrooms, teachers will be paired in teams. You will meet your students at your assigned spots. Parents are outside, but I advise you not to talk to them. If a reporter approaches, don't speak to him. There are some concerns about the high school. It's possible that police will be called in to assure a safe and orderly transition."

"More police?" a teacher called from one of the tables, breaking the silence.

A bell buzzed in the hallway.

"Teachers, there's the eight o'clock bell. Please go meet your students," Mr. Palmer said.

Colleen followed the white teachers and observed their routine of standing with a class sign along the back walkway. The building hid the demonstrations from the gathering children.

Colleen scanned the yard for familiar faces. "Lulu! There you are! Have you seen Evelyn?"

Lulu stared ahead, gritted her teeth, and hardly moved her lips as she spoke. "Didn't you hear, Colleen? I don't have a class anymore. You get six of mine. I get to 'help out.' And maybe you shouldn't talk to me."

"What?" Colleen whispered.

A white teacher glared at her. Lulu nodded toward the back

of the building. Evelyn was standing with her 3C sign. A line of brown faces stood behind her. Colleen's heart thumped with the sudden realization that the lines behind the white teachers had white children first, with a few black faces at the ends. She searched the faces of her students and realized how quiet they were. *They're scared to death.*

A quick head count told her one was missing. Turning, she recognized one of her students approaching with a tall, broad-shouldered boy.

"Good morning, Rachel! Is this your brother?"

Rachel's eyes darted from her teacher to the class behind her. *Even she won't speak to me.*

"Yes, ma'am. I'm Frank."

"You can meet us here at dismissal, Frank. I hope you have a good day." Colleen took Rachel's shaking hand. "Come here, sweetie. Stand with me."

As Colleen watched Rachel's brother walk away, she wished she had spoken to him a bit more. He appeared worried. She watched him as he walked toward the high school, his pace hurried. She turned back to her line and counted thirty students.

"Children! Everyone is here. Let's go see our new classroom. Please follow me."

As Colleen walked her class toward the trailer, she threw her shoulders back and held her head high. Would she be able to stay and do this? She had never quit a job. Her throat tightened. She was having trouble breathing.

On the periphery of her vision, a figure moved quickly. Was that Rachel's brother, Frank, running? In the street, a policeman struggled to keep a dog from leaping toward some girls. Colleen hurried to usher the class into the trailer, locking the door from the inside.

Chapter 16

❧

Frank

Wednesday, November 5, 1969

As Frank passed the line of white folks, they were pointing to a crowd of students gathering on the side of the white high school across the street. He recognized Sissy's friends Pearl and Kendra walking toward his sister, who was still standing where he had left her.

Frank looked around and noticed a tall white man with a camera. He was speaking to a policeman and writing something down. Other men with notebooks and pencils stood on the sidewalk.

Across the street, a police dog growled at Sissy, Pearl, and Kendra. The dog lunged forward, and the officer with the leash pulled back hard, lifting the animal's front legs into the air. The dog reared up higher, barking wildly, showing its sharp teeth. Sissy and her friends stumbled away, terror on their faces.

Sissy rushed toward him. "Frank! That dog tried to get us! We don't know where to go."

Her mouth quivered, and he put his hand on her shoulder. "Don't worry," he said. "I'll help you find your teacher." The three girls followed him into the school. He led them to some teachers set up at tables, handing out student schedules.

Frank turned and plowed his way through students anxious to enter the building. He ran to the back of the school as if he had just been handed the football on his way to a touchdown. The door to the gym was open. His varsity team, the JV team, and the cheerleaders sat high up in the bleachers. As he made his way to his friends, he saw that only Negro students were at the meeting.

He scanned the far court. "Where's Coach?"

"Not here yet," the quarterback replied. "Here comes Peterson."

Dressed in his typical suit and tie, Mr. Peterson made an impressive entrance. He walked across the far court to join the coaches and a man Frank didn't know.

The students chattered nervously as they waited.

"Have you ever seen a gym like this one?"

"Is that a double basketball court?"

Five coaches stood in a line facing the students. Each had a whistle attached to a lanyard around his neck, a blue-collared knit shirt, khaki shorts, white socks, and gym shoes. Hands clasped behind their backs, they looked like they were posing for a photograph.

Seeing Mr. Peterson, one of the white coaches blew his whistle to get the students' attention. He grew impatient and blew it again. Frank realized that the meeting was starting without their head football coach.

The white coach told them his name was Coach Welborn. "Good morning. Welcome to Kettle Creek High School." Then he introduced the other two white coaches as his assistants and asked them to pass out the rosters.

"Next to your name, you will see that you have all kept your positions and will remain on the varsity team, but as second string to Kettle Creek High School's team."

Frank sat in stunned silence as his teammates gasped and shouted.

"Second string?"

"Where's our coach?"

"Why can't we play?"

One of the seniors called out, "We can't go to our own school, and now we can't play here?"

Coach Welborn blew his whistle. "You still have these coaches." He pointed at the black coaches. "Y'all get scrimmages."

The quarterback stood up and walked down to the gym floor. That was the signal.

Sixty students stood.

"Hey! Where y'all going?"

"Stop! Sit back down!"

The students ignored the coaches' whistles and walked out of the gym.

As he passed the line of men, Frank heard Coach Welborn say, "Hey, Peterson! What just happened?"

Another white coach said, "You need to discipline those colored kids."

Fred Peterson stood strong, his shoulders back, his fisted hands at his sides. "Did you really expect that they would just go along with it?"

Mr. Peterson and Mr. Armstrong, the other assistant principal, walked outside. The students were seated on the grass. As they approached the group, Dedra, West Hill School's student council president, stood to speak.

"Mr. Peterson, we want representation on the football team, the cheerleading squad, and the student council."

Mr. Peterson's eyes scanned the group and then returned to Dedra. "Young lady, I understand that, but this isn't the way it will happen. Classes have started, and you need to go into the building or leave the school property."

Mr. Peterson pulled at the knot of his tie as Dedra nodded at her fellow students. They rose on her cue.

Frank felt the energy of the crowd of black students as they walked off the field in defiance. Their voices might have been silenced, but their feet spoke volumes. The pounding of shoes on the pavement caught the attention of the people holding the FREEDOM OF CHOICE signs, who watched in astonishment.

Freedom of choice, Frank wanted to call out. *Guess that's what we're doing now.*

Mouths tight, eyes focused straight ahead, Frank and his friends walked down the middle of the street—past the police, the reporters, the elementary school. Arms and legs swung in time to an internal drumbeat, filling him with energy while they moved along as one.

At first the police seemed stunned, but they pulled out their bullhorns and shouted for the students to halt. Dogs barked nearby. A girl screamed.

As they reached the second intersection about half a mile down the street, the persistent barking of the dogs and the police bullhorns' blaring shouts to halt created even more confusion. Frank was no longer in the center of the crowd. The students behind Frank broke into a run. Patrol cars blocked the road behind them. Police flooded the street before them. Dogs snarled. They were surrounded.

Someone tackled Frank from behind. He struggled to rise, but the weight of a boot held him in place. Stones from the street pressed into his cheek. His arms were yanked back, and handcuffs clicked around his wrists. He thought of his mother.

The person grabbed Frank's shirt to pull him up and looked him in the eye—an officer, his face purple with anger. "Don't want no trouble from you, boy! Don't you be like your daddy, now!"

Frank felt boneless with shock at the unexpected mention of his father and the hate he saw in those eyes. He tried to jerk free as the officer shoved him into another handcuffed classmate. Other students shouted while dogs chased them. The police slung billy clubs along with muttered curses and racial slurs. Frank tasted his own fear as bile rose into his mouth. Flashes of color raced past him in the confusion of the moment, and his mind raced to another time.

That was when Frank recognized the officer. Years ago, this man had ticketed cars and trucks that came to the repair shop Frank's father owned. His father had tried talking to the officer, but the conversation had turned heated. Frank's father paid the tickets himself so he didn't lose his customers.

The handcuffs' cold metal bit into Frank's wrists.

Chapter 17

✿

Evelyn

Wednesday, November 5, 1969

"Come in!" Evelyn shouted.

The morning of the first day at Kettle Creek Elementary School had passed without incident, and it was almost time for lunch.

The knocking continued.

"Come in!"

Now someone was pounding. The students were wide-eyed. Evelyn interrupted her lesson, walking through the narrow row between desks and wondering what was so important that she had to go to the trailer door. When she opened it, a tall white student shoved a paper at her and left without speaking.

Guess he didn't want to come into a colored classroom.

Evelyn's stomach clenched as she read the note.

Teachers:

There has been a problem at the high school. Do not leave your classrooms until your assigned lunchtime. Escort your students to the cafeteria in an orderly manner.

The lunch aides will keep the students indoors for recess. Do not discuss this information with your classes.

Mr. Palmer, Principal

Evelyn scanned the area outside the open door of her mobile classroom. A gentle breeze rustled the trees beneath a cloudless blue sky. The street was empty. All police, reporters, and parents were gone. What was the problem?

She closed the door with a gentle tug, wishing it had a window. When she turned, thirty pairs of questioning eyes greeted her. One boy bravely raised his hand, and she nodded at him.

"Ms. Glover, what he done give you? Are we movin' agin?"

"No, child, nothing like that. Just directions on how to get to the cafeteria. You must be getting hungry. We can line up inside now, and then I'll take you there. Doesn't that sound good?"

She hated lying, even with the goal of protecting her students.

Once her class was safely situated in the cafeteria, Evelyn spotted Lulu walking in the opposite direction.

"Lulu, where are you going?"

"Don't know. No one told me where to eat."

Lulu looked distraught. Her fitted shirtwaist dress appeared to be the only thing holding her together.

"The teachers' lunchroom. Follow me."

As they walked, Lulu wouldn't stop talking. "I'm an aide in a class. Supposed to be a teacher, but they don't let me do anything. Then I had to cover another class so the teacher could have a break. A break! To use the bathroom! Don't know where *our* bathroom is."

She kept it up, even when they entered the lunchroom full of teachers they didn't know. The white teachers were whispering to one another: "How unruly are your new ones?" "Is that smell from their hair?"

Still, Lulu wouldn't stop complaining.

"Hush, now." Evelyn gave her friend a gentle nudge with her arm.

"Oh no—two more," one of the white teachers whispered too loudly.

"Are they going to use our dishes?" another murmured.

Lulu didn't seem to notice, or if she did, it didn't stop her from talking. "Well, aren't you the one—Evelyn Glover, hand-picked to keep your class."

Evelyn gritted her teeth, feeling the eyes of the white teachers on her. "Let's talk about it later."

They joined a table of black teachers in the back of the room. Evelyn's chair wobbled, and she saw that one of the plastic caps on the legs was missing.

Lulu continued to mumble. "Lordy, least they gave us a table inside."

Evelyn thought about the previous day, which felt a world away by now. As the men with clipboards had left her class-room, she had overheard Mr. Palmer tell Mr. Peterson, "If I have to take all these teachers, I want only the best to keep their classes."

Lulu gasped and poked Evelyn in the ribs, bringing her back to the present moment. What had finally made Lulu stop complaining?

It was Colleen, sitting down at the same table of white teachers who had been so rude.

A blond ponytail swished as the teacher at the end of the table stood up and said, "Same here, darlin'—don't think we need Yankees helping us with our coloreds."

A fierce blush rose on Colleen's face, hiding her freckles.

Colleen bit her lip and stared down at her brown paper lunch bag.

Well, that girl has her own troubles, doesn't she?

At the end of the day, Lulu came to Evelyn's classroom trailer. Her easy laugh was gone, and her eyelids were puffy. Wide circles of perspiration marked her underarms. Lulu's class had been divided up into the other second grades. Six in Colleen's, and a new white teacher got the rest. What was Lulu supposed to do now?

"Look here, now, Lu. Don't let them beat you down," Evelyn said. But she felt a quiet guilt. She was proud to have been chosen to keep her class, but did that pride betray her friend?

Lulu shook her head. "You saw what those white teachers did to Colleen at lunch. White women usually say mean things in a sweet voice with a smile on their face. Today, they didn't even bother to smile."

Evelyn shrugged. "Colleen can deal with her own kind. She must know how to handle them."

"Do you hear yourself? Colleen's no better off than we are."

"I can't worry about a white woman." Evelyn opened a drawer to her desk, staring down into it. She couldn't remember what she was looking for.

Lulu tugged at the buttons on her shirtdress. "It's hot in here, Evie. I can hardly get a breath."

"I turned off the air conditioner because these poor babies were cold. They're not used to it."

Lulu walked to the back and turned it on, letting the blower wick the sweat trickling down her neck.

"Humph. Feels good to me."

Evelyn frowned. "I told them to bring a sweater or wear a long-sleeved shirt tomorrow."

"You've got no worries, Evelyn Glover. Know what I had to put up with today? Is this a hundred years ago?"

Evelyn searched for the right thing to say. Lulu was a kind soul who visited her students at home if they took ill. Her desk and bookshelves had been cluttered with cherished treasures from years of teaching second-graders. She even saved hand-made creations of pipe cleaners and Popsicle sticks licked clean.

"Tell me about it. I'm listening."

"Those white teachers got special meetings on how to integrate our children into their classes, but no one could bother telling me where I could eat my lunch."

"I'm so sorry."

"And the white teachers keep complaining." Lulu sat on a student's desk and said, in a high, whiny voice, "'What are we supposed to do with these children? Why did they close the colored schools now?'"

"I guess that's the one thing we agree on with the white teachers. Why now?" Evelyn walked over to the air conditioner to turn down the blower. "We should have been included in the meeting. Remember, if we don't do well, the principal can transfer us."

Lulu scowled. "For what? Do you see any white faces in your classroom? And where will they send me, Evie? I'm at the bottom now. There's no place lower for me to go."

Chapter 18

●

Colleen

Wednesday, November 5, 1969

As she parked her car, Colleen saw Miguel standing on the dirt road, talking to Jan. Her hand was on one hip as she wagged her finger at him. When he stepped back, she stepped forward. Colleen leaned over the steering wheel and sighed, wishing she had been able to tell Miguel about the day first.

Colleen sat there, exhausted, hoping Jan would go inside. No such luck—Jan strutted to the car and tapped on the window.

"Oh my—you're late getting back. And it's your first day in the white school! I'm glad to work in a private school where we don't have to deal with this nonsense. I don't know how you can do it—all day in that trailer classroom with those colored kids. You must need to take a shower as soon as you get home."

How can she say such things? Colleen threw open the car door, narrowly missing Jan.

"It was a long day, and I'm tired. I need to make dinner. Let's catch up another time."

Colleen clutched her schoolbag and scrambled to her trailer, leaving Jan standing there. She was grateful that Miguel had arrived home first and cooled the trailer. The drone of the air conditioner muffled the sobs that escaped from her the instant she shut the door.

When Miguel came in, she tried to talk but choked on the words. He held her close, stroking her hair. *"Mi amor, lo siento.* I'm sorry."

His tender words only made her cry harder. She pulled away from him, hiding her face in her hands.

"Colleen, we can talk later, whenever you want. Let's just eat the leftover meat loaf for supper and then see how you feel."

Lying on their bed, she listened to Miguel as he began busying himself in the kitchen and wondered what she had gotten herself into. In three months at West Hill School, she had adjusted and—aside from some moments of tension with Evelyn—felt welcomed. She'd grown fond of her students. But each night had been an abrupt transfer back into her comfortable white world. Now the white world was foreign, unfamiliar, and judgmental.

Her first day with her students at the new school had gone better than she'd anticipated. The portable classroom was a novelty, and they were excited about the new notebooks and crayons that Colleen had purchased as emergency supplies for the overnight move. The classroom's tight quarters served as a cocoon, protecting them from the confusion of the schoolyard and the activity on the street across from the high school.

But then there was lunch.

The teachers' lounge had been crowded. In the front, the tables were decorated with small vases of flowers, napkins, and pairs of salt and pepper shakers, like at Colleen's favorite pizza parlor back home. But the black teachers all sat at card tables with folding chairs in the back of the room. She had lifted her hand to wave at Lulu and Evelyn but hesitated, remembering Lulu's coolness earlier in the day. Their table was full anyway.

Spotting an empty place at one of the front tables, she asked if the seat was taken. No one looked up or answered her. So she sat down across from a woman who was busy putting away a small makeup case. Her blond hair was styled in a pageboy, which she had just smoothed down after a look in her compact mirror. Colleen envied the woman's freckle-free, alabaster complexion.

Colleen said, "Hello."

The teacher didn't respond, so Colleen figured she hadn't heard her and greeted the woman a second time. "Hi, my name is Colleen Rodriguez. What's yours?"

No reply.

Colleen was seated directly across from the woman, who looked straight into her eyes. How could she not have heard her?

"What grade do you teach?" asked Colleen.

No reply.

Colleen felt a chill creep up her back. The woman looked right through her. She was stone-faced, an unfinished sculpture, devoid of expression.

It was as if the chair Colleen had chosen were still vacant.

A teacher from the end of the table confirmed Colleen's feeling.

"She won't waste her time talking to you. Same here, darlin'—don't think we need Yankees helping us with our coloreds."

The affront stung as if the teacher had slapped Colleen's face. As she reached into her brown bag, her hands shook. Her favorite tuna salad on pumpernickel bread was no longer appealing. A knot of anxiety twisted her stomach. She looked at her watch and realized that she had forty minutes before she

84

needed to return to her classroom. The gift of lunch without playground duty had become a penalty.

An older woman retrieved a whistling teakettle. When she returned to her place, she asked if anyone would like a cup of tea. Her cat's-eye glasses framed her large green eyes. She nodded and smiled when Colleen looked back.

"Thank you, but I don't have a cup."

"Well, I'm sure we can rinse one out for you," the teacher said.

A mutter came from the opposite end of the table. "She wouldn't mind a dirty cup."

The older teacher ignored the remark and cleaned a cup for Colleen. That single act of kindness helped her through the rest of the meal.

In the trailer, Miguel called from the kitchen that dinner was ready. Colleen smiled, grateful for the warmth and comfort of his presence. She went to the bathroom sink and rinsed the dried tears from her eyes. She threw her shoulders back and stood tall as she felt a reserve of courage rise and move through her.

She wouldn't let that alabaster statue keep *her* out of the lunchroom.

Chapter 19

♥

Evelyn

Wednesday, November 5, 1969

E velyn knocked on Annie Mae Woods's door. They had
planned to go to a meeting about the school closing at the
church hall.

The dead bolt slid, and the door opened wide.

"Hello, Sissy. Is your mama ready?"

Sissy stepped back without answering and gestured toward
her mother, who stood in the kitchen. She had just put the
phone back on the hook.

"What's wrong?" Evelyn asked.

"Frank's not home yet. Something happened." Annie Mae's
face clouded with worry. "He claimed to have an early football
practice, but I knew it wasn't true. He overslept, and I delayed
him more by asking him to take his sisters to school."

"Yes, I saw him walking Rachel to her line," said Evelyn.

"But he didn't meet her after school. It's not like him,
Evelyn."

Worry surged through Evelyn's body.

"Annie Mae, there was a problem in the morning at the

high school. We got a note to keep the children inside at recess. That's all I heard."

"A problem? What kind of problem?"

"I'm sorry, but I don't know. All the reporters and the folks with signs were gone when we walked into the school at lunchtime."

"Reporters? Signs?" Annie Mae clutched her hands to her chest. "Sissy, why didn't you tell me?"

"I'm sorry, Mama. I didn't want to get you upset. Frank took Pearl and me into school after the dog scared us."

"A dog? Sissy! What else?"

"Come to the meeting," Evelyn said. "Leave Sissy with Rachel and bring James along. The reverend might know more."

Annie Mae hesitated but then nodded.

The church's heavy door creaked when Evelyn pushed it open. The reverend was sorting pamphlets beneath a large, arched window. She caught his worried expression before he managed to mask it.

"Good evening, Evelyn, Annie Mae—and look at this fine boy. Hello, James. Why, doesn't he look just like his daddy, God rest his soul."

"Good evening, Reverend," Evelyn said. "Can we help you with that?"

"No, no. Praise to God, and have a seat in His house. I believe we'll wait for the others before I share the news."

Alarm spread over Annie Mae's face.

Evelyn spoke first. "Reverend, Frank hasn't come home from school yet. Do you know something about that?"

"Frank? No, I didn't hear—"

The church door flew open with such force that it blew the

pamphlets the reverend had just sorted. Evelyn wasn't surprised to see their friend Mavis enter. Her grand entrance almost knocked off the smooth pixie-style wig she insisted on wearing. Mavis didn't mean to attract attention, but she always did.

"Evening, Reverend. Evening, Evelyn. And Annie Mae—hoo, hoo! Look at James! Not a baby anymore. Those hands, those feet. Like a puppy, he is. He'll grow into 'em. Be bigger than your boy Frank. No one can get past Frank on the field. Best fullback this town has ever seen!"

A stream of people followed Mavis, filling the church with energy and concern. Men came in their overalls from the tire factory, women in their maids' uniforms, and civilian clerks from the army base in their tidy suits and skirts.

Evelyn counted more than thirty people. She could see that they were all feeling the day's heat as she wiped her own brow. The hard wooden pews didn't provide much comfort, either.

Reverend Wilford stood at the front of the room. "Welcome to the Lord's house. Let's begin with a prayer."

Pray hard, Evelyn thought. *Pray for wisdom. Pray for peace.*

After the prayer, the reverend looked uncomfortable and pulled at his white collar, as if to let some steam out. "Good people, Mr. Peterson came to speak to me last night. He has concerns over some decisions beyond his control.

"As you know, today is the first day that our children were placed in the white school. We will face challenges, but the first is our football team. Rumor has it that the coaches of the white team are putting our players in as second string."

Annie Mae gasped. All eyes turned toward her.

Mavis shouted what everyone was thinking: "Frank is counting on that football scholarship! What about the Thanksgiving game?"

The reverend pulled at his collar again. He spoke slowly. "All that I can tell you now is that Mr. Peterson and I are meeting with the coaches to try to resolve this issue."

Everyone started talking, finishing each other's thoughts.

"Reverend, you know this is going to get hot."

"We might hear things, but . . ."

"Doubtful we can stop it."

Evelyn didn't miss how Annie Mae tried to hide her tears by sneezing into her handkerchief.

The reverend cleared his throat. "We don't want anyone to get into trouble or get hurt. We must learn from what happened in other towns. Back in August, there was a fight at the New Egypt High School."

People shook their heads, muttering.

"There was a riot—colored against whites."

"The police teargassed the colored students."

"Two hundred arrested."

The room fell silent as the church door creaked open again. One of the high school cheerleaders burst in. She shouted, "Six students have been arrested! Miz Woods, Sissy told me you were here. Frank needs you at the police station."

Evelyn gasped as she looked at Annie Mae.

Pray for wisdom.

Chapter 20

🍎

Frank

Thursday, November 6, 1969

Frank shifted his weight, watching Mr. Peterson approach the glass-walled main office. Perched on the edge of an upholstered chair, his mother faced Frank but gazed past him. Her mouth was snapped shut, and her eyes were puffed.

After his mother had brought him home the night before, he knew she had gone back to finish the ironing she'd brought home from work. And this morning she must have been up at the crack of dawn because his breakfast had been on the table, waiting for him, as usual.

She hadn't spoken to him since she'd picked him up at the police station, except to say, "Are you ready? We have to meet with Mr. Peterson by eight thirty."

Teachers walked past Frank, and some hurried out the office door. Frank couldn't see behind the counter, but he knew that was where the secretary had her desk. He heard a teacher call the secretary Millie.

Frank could see Mr. Peterson through the glass office wall. He kept stopping to speak to groups of students, *all* the students. Frank imagined the greetings. He'd been on the receiving end often enough.

Good morning. You're looking fine today, Frank.

How is your mama?

Great game you had last week.

After Mr. Peterson left the last group of white students, they broke into laughter. One of them saluted the retreating principal.

Frank's heart skipped when Mr. Peterson finally entered the main office. "Good day, Mrs. Woods, Frank. We can meet in here." He started to open a door to a smaller office.

Millie jumped up and shook her head in disapproval. "Mr. Peterson, may I help you? Mr. Armstrong isn't in his office." She stepped in front of Mr. Peterson, blocking his way.

"Yes, I know. I'm going to use his office this morning for some meetings. My next appointment is at nine o'clock."

Millie put one hand on the doorknob and the other on her hip. "Well, this is quite unusual. Mr. Armstrong didn't mention that to me."

Mr. Peterson towered over the secretary, but his height and stature gave her no pause.

"Millie, until I have a full-size office, Joe and I will be sharing his. Didn't he tell you that he would be meeting with the student council members this morning?"

"Yes, and I was going to do some filing for him. His desk is piled high with reports."

Peterson held eye contact with Millie.

"When I see Mr. Armstrong later this morning, I'll tell him that you weren't able to do that. I won't disturb the reports."

Millie moved aside, still shaking her head. Mr. Peterson reached past her to usher his visitors inside.

The mess on Mr. Armstrong's desk surprised Frank. Atop

one pile of files was a half-eaten donut and a mug of coffee. He knew his mother wouldn't approve of the careless jumble. Mr. Peterson sat them at a small, clean table surrounded by several chairs.

Every time Frank looked at his mother, he felt the blood rush through his veins. She had her light cotton coat with the wide collar buttoned over her maid's uniform. He wondered which of the white ladies she cleaned for was waiting for her. She wouldn't get a full day's pay today.

On the other side of the glass door, Millie held her telephone to her ear. She was gesturing broadly with her free hand, and her face was blazing. Frank clenched his jaw. If Mr. Peterson wasn't respected in this school, then what hope did any of the black students have?

Mr. Peterson began the meeting: "Well, Frank, I don't recall ever having you in my office back at West Hill School."

"No, sir, you never did."

"Your mama must be upset, and I appreciate her presence here today, but you're the one I will speak to. Do you understand that when you left school property it amounted to cutting school?"

"Yes, sir." Frank shifted in his chair and leaned forward, gripping its arms.

"So why did you do it?"

"Mr. Peterson, it's not fair. If I can't play football, I lose my chance for a scholarship. I'm just as good as any of those white kids. Maybe better!"

He started to rise from his seat. His mother touched his arm, and he sat back down.

"Frank, your mama and I are on your side. We need to hear your story. Where were you going when you walked off the field?"

"Some of the guys wanted to walk to our old school. We didn't have much of a plan. I guess we panicked when we saw the police cars blocking the street. We started running."

"What did your mama say when she came to get you from the police station?"

Frank turned to his mother and saw tears filling her eyes. Guilt soured his stomach.

"She didn't say anything to me. The cops told her if I caused any more trouble, they would put me in a cell and lose the key." He leaned back with his head down and his shoulders slumped.

"You know they could do worse," Peterson said gently.

Frank's voice rose. "I know what worse is. My daddy learned what worse was. I want to get out of this town. Maybe I should just quit and join the army."

Neither of them spoke for a while.

Eventually, Mr. Peterson broke the silence. "The army won't solve everything. It wasn't easy for me to come home from the Korean War to a country that didn't respect me. It wasn't easy then, and it's not easy now."

Frank wanted to punch a hole through the wall at the unfairness of it all. "I don't know if I can be like you or my daddy," he muttered. "Look how that secretary treated you out there."

A surprised look crossed Peterson's face. "And who won that one? Son, your mama needs you to keep a level head now. Reverend Wilford and I will help you and the rest of the students as best we can, but I need your help."

Frank sat up straighter. "How can I help, Mr. Peterson?"

"You weren't a leader in this, but you got arrested. The police have dropped the charges, but, like they told you, no more trouble. So, for now, that's what I'm asking. Can you do that?"

Frank nodded. Tears glistened in his mother's eyes, and her lips were pursed, as if to keep any words within. He never knew her not to speak her mind. What would she think if she knew he had recognized the officer who had arrested him the day before?

"Don't want no trouble from you, boy! Don't you be like your daddy, now!"

Frank rubbed his wrists. They were bruised from the jostling and the handcuffs. The memory of those words sent a chill through him.

That night in his bedroom, he pulled the second drawer out of his bureau, placed it on the bed, and reached into the hiding space he'd used for years. His fingers found something cool and metallic: the lighter he'd discovered at the scene of the fire that had killed his father.

Frank turned over the lighter to study the engraved monogram. He opened and closed the cap. *Click, click, click, click, click*—it was obsessive. The sound made him remember the *clink-clink* of the handcuffs each time he had shifted in the jail cell.

A memory bubbled up. He pushed it away.

Could he keep his promise to Peterson? Maybe, but only for his mother. Frank wanted to take care of her just as she took care of him. How was he going to get into college, get a good job, and make enough money to do that someday? Without a scholarship, he wouldn't be able to. He couldn't disappoint her like this again.

As he clasped his hands to flex his wrists, imagination collided with memory.

Clink, clink, clink. Metal against metal.

Handcuffs.

Lighter.

He felt his throat close.

That officer who'd arrested him—Frank had seen him years

94

earlier, shortly after the fire, searching in the grass outside his daddy's gutted shop. Frank had hoped it was part of an investigation, but nothing had come of it. And the cop had hurried to the patrol car when he saw Frank approach.

Frank knew the police didn't care about his side of town or about the fire. So why had the cop been there? There weren't any cars to ticket at that point.

Was he looking for this lighter?

Chapter 21

🍎

Colleen

Saturday, November 22, 1969

"Miguel, please. I promised them."

Reluctantly, he handed over the car keys. "Can't you wait till things calm down? Is it safe for you to do this alone?"

"Do one thing every day that scares you. That's what Eleanor Roosevelt told me."

"Huh? When did she tell you that?"

Colleen rolled her eyes. "It's a joke. But that's what my grandmother used to say. She quoted her favorite first lady a lot."

"Then you admit that you're scared?" Miguel asked.

"A bit nervous, maybe, but I'm going to do it. I'm taking those children to the library. I'll be back by noon."

As she drove, Colleen remembered how excited Cynthia had been the day before: "Miz Rodriguez! It's my turn tomorrow, right? My mama gave me the paper. You gonna pick me up? It's my turn."

It was their third Saturday monthly trip to the library and the first since everyone had been uprooted from West Hill School. Distracted by her thoughts, Colleen almost missed her turn. As she drove past her old school into the Negro neighborhood, the road narrowed until it was barely wide enough for two cars to pass. There was a runoff ditch on either side. She drove over a huge pipe. It served as the foundation of the entrance to the dirt road and funneled any water that was in the ditch. She was sure she had seen some animal, maybe an alligator, crawling into it a mile or so back. It was the road that Cynthia and Linkston lived on.

The houses were set behind huge trees with Spanish moss dripping from the branches, like curtains shielding the lives of the tenants. Life was different here for sure. She passed a house with an upholstered armchair on the porch, another with an old wringer washing machine in the corner. Most were just weathered wood, not as well tended as the Negro houses closer to town and school. She drove slowly, remembering what Cynthia had said about her house. "We just put the white paint on. It looks good!"

Colleen felt her heart pounding as she passed a man sweeping the gravel and stray twigs back to the road. He stared at her, and she realized her car had knocked some stones back into his garden. He was a big, dark man with a bald head and huge brown eyes rimmed in white.

Colleen stopped the car. Behind the man, two children ran toward her, bubbling with laughter: Cynthia and Linkston.

Colleen stepped out to greet them.

"Granddaddy," Cynthia said. "This is our teacher."

"Good morning, sir. I'm sorry about the gravel." Colleen felt herself flush.

After a long pause, he limped over to meet her. "Mornin', miss. Everyone calls me Ole Man Everett, but I'm not that old." He squinted at her. "I graduated high school with that principal of yours, Freddy Peterson." He studied her car. "That's a might fancy machine you gots there. You aiming to take these youngins somewhere?"

Colleen didn't know what to say. Cynthia saved her. "Granddaddy, she gonna take Linkston and me to the library. It's our turn."

Colleen introduced herself to Cynthia's mother, who had approached from the house. The woman hesitated before shaking Colleen's outstretched hand. "Pleased to meet you, Miz Rodriguez. I'm Chantal Everett. I see you met my father, Joseph Everett."

Cynthia's mother was younger than Colleen had expected. Her hair was pulled back smoothly, with a headband holding down any strays. She wore a uniform, clean and pressed, just like Cynthia's dresses were every day.

"I'm very glad to meet you. Thank you for signing the permission for the library card for Cynthia."

"Well, I thank you. Cynthia has been reading more than she ever did. She wasn't interested until this year. You know, it's her second time in 2C."

Colleen didn't know and didn't want to admit it. She nodded, smiling, as she looked around for the other two children. Rachel and Jarrod were supposed to meet her here too.

"Miz Rodriguez, I have some news." Eyes down, Cynthia's mother nervously smoothed the pocket of her skirt. "The other children won't be coming. Miz Woods sends her apologies, but Rachel and her cousin Jarrod have family business today."

Colleen wondered if the family business had anything to do with Frank. The day before, Rachel had confessed that her brother had been arrested.

"But are Cynthia and Linkston able to go with me?"

The children were jumping up to peer into the car, obviously anxious to get inside.

"Yes, they can go. I have work today, but Cynthia's grand-daddy will be here when you bring them back."

"Thank you. I'll have them back by eleven thirty."

As Colleen opened the passenger door and pulled the seat forward, both children scrambled into the back and fastened their seat belts. She laughed to herself. She had explained that there were seat belts just like the astronauts wore in the space shuttle to the moon. And she thought of her own reluctance to wear a seat belt because it wrinkled her miniskirt.

Why had Mrs. Woods changed her mind without notice? She had been the one parent Colleen thought she could count on and the first to sign for the library cards. The others had followed. And Cynthia's granddaddy didn't seem especially pleased. Because she had knocked stones back into his garden, or was it something else?

During the drive, Cynthia chattered away, commenting on everything in view.

"Miz Rodriguez, look at that there park. I never saw it before."

Linkston broke his silence to say, "Can we go? Can we go there too?"

"Yeah. There are swings and a big slide, and no one is using it," Cynthia added.

"I think the park is locked, children. We won't be able to play there. You want to spend time inside the library, don't you?"

Colleen knew the town had closed the park, put a lock on the gate so it wouldn't have to be integrated. Evelyn told her that had happened sometime the prior year. *Deny everyone so you don't have to share*, Colleen thought.

She parked in the lot next to the library. She knew from

experience that there would be stares, whispers, and finger pointing at the sight of a white woman holding hands with some black kids. But Eleanor Roosevelt's words echoed in her mind.

The head librarian, Mrs. Meriwether, sat at the main desk. The children didn't notice the eyes piercing the air as they walked in. One glance was all Colleen needed to see that the beehive was in place, pulling back any wrinkle that dared to appear on the librarian's face.

Colleen led Cynthia and Linkston to the Children's Room. The young librarian with the dark brown pageboy read to a group of children seated at a table. There were some open seats, and the three of them sat down to listen to the story. One of the girls wiggled her fingers in a greeting to Cynthia and smiled at her. Another child moved her chair away from the table and made a face at the friendly girl.

When the librarian finished the book, she suggested that the children look for more by the same author on the shelf behind her. Cynthia jumped up to see. Colleen quickly followed, dragging Linkston along.

"Hi," the young librarian said to Colleen. "I remember you. Is there something I can help your children with?"

Colleen smiled back at the woman's twinkle-eyed face. Maybe this could work out. She explained that Cynthia loved books about dogs and Linkston preferred anything about outer space.

When the young librarian checked out the books Cynthia and Linkston had chosen, she said, "Children, please return the books in one month, either here or to your school."

"To their school?" Colleen asked.

"They go to Kettle Creek School now, don't they? We have a pickup directly from the school library. Just be sure to place the books in our bin. Your school librarian will help you."

Colleen smiled. *A chink in the wall.*

◆◆◆

As she drove the children home, Colleen thought about how well the trip had gone. It had been the best trip to the library that she had taken yet. Miguel had been worried for nothing.

The children flipped happily through the piles of books they held on their laps. Colleen drove them to Cynthia's house, and Mr. Everett acknowledged their return with a smile and a wave as he started walking toward the grove of trees that separated the highway from the road.

Just as Colleen left the gravel road and entered the high-way, a police car flashed its lights behind her. She couldn't pull over to let it pass because of the ditch, but she was able to move onto a narrow shoulder a little farther down. Instead of passing her, the patrol car pulled up and parked behind her. The officer climbed out of the car and approached. His trousers were pegged, and he had on knee-high leather boots. The state troopers in New Jersey dressed like that.

Colleen frowned, uncertain what she'd done wrong.

"Morning, ma'am. License and registration, please."

Colleen's hands shook as she reached over to the glove box for the registration. Her purse was on the floor, and she couldn't reach it without taking off her seat belt. As she leaned over, she felt her skirt slide up.

I can't believe this.

Handing over her documents, she noticed that the officer's forearm was scarred. Then she read his nameplate: Beau Harper. She saw him look at her legs as she wiggled to fix her skirt. Beau? Wasn't that the name of the so-called best mechanic in Kettle Creek?

"So, you get around in this fancy car. Are you lost?"

"No, Officer, I'm not lost."

"What's a pretty thing like you doing way out here?"

Dark green aviator sunglasses hid his eyes, and she couldn't work out his expression.

"I'm a teacher—"

He didn't let her finish. "A teacher, now? Is that right? Last time I saw this car, you needed a hose replaced."

So it *was* the mechanic. But he was a cop too?

"Officer, did I do something wrong?"

"Well, now, that depends. Why would a white woman be out driving in these parts?"

"I took some of my students to the library, and then I drove them home."

He palmed her cards and walked to look at the front of the car.

"New Jersey—you're far from home." His tone challenged her. "There's no library out here."

Colleen felt her throat constrict. She needed air. *Breathe.*

"I took them to the library in Kettle Creek."

Scrutinizing her identification, he rested his hand on his hip above his holster. She heard a creak as the leather strained across the pistol.

"No teacher of mine ever took me to the library. Are you collecting signatures or something?"

"Signatures? What for?"

He handed Colleen her license and registration.

"Little lady, you're far from home and don't belong down these roads. We've had some nonsense with some of the church ladies coming out this way with their northern people, signing up the coloreds to vote. Don't come this way again, you hear? Or else you'll find this is a heap of trouble you know nothing about."

Chapter 22

❡

Frank

Sunday, November 23, 1969

I t had been a long time since Frank had been in the storage shed at the back of the yard, but it wasn't far enough from the house. He could still hear his mama shouting, "Franklin Delano Woods, don't you be sassing me. You get on, now—get yourself busy."

Sissy shouldn't have told Mama anything.

He had to go find the things he needed to fix his mama's car.

Where is that creeper?

The shelves were still organized as they had been when his father had died. As he looked around, he saw tightly sealed, partially used cans of paint, a jug of turpentine evaporating from the heat, a tin of car wax, and his father's favorite chamois, the one he had used for the car's final shine. Frank picked up the polishing cloth and inhaled the wax left on it. He could feel his father's presence. *Damn, this place smells like him.*

The back of the shed had an old motor, stacked tires, two rusty bikes, and a wheelbarrow, all waiting for someone to use or repair them. His father liked to fix things. Frank didn't.

This is just a bunch of junk. Where's that creeper?

Frank spotted the flat wooden top with the padded leather headrest behind the wheelbarrow. It was long enough for him to lie on and maneuver with his feet dangling off one end. It stood on its end, so he could read the black-lettered inscription as clearly as the first time he'd seen it: SMASH-PROOF AUTO CREEPER.

Just what I need—smash-proof.

He couldn't believe Sissy had told his mother that he'd been caught slamming the locker doors left open in the locker room. Head Coach Welborn had wanted to know why he was so angry.

What is he, an idiot?

The old '53 Ford Victoria was leaking oil badly. His parents had bought the car when it was ten years old from Auntie Penelope, who rarely drove it. But his mother used it every day, and she had been after Frank to see about it, especially since he had time after school now.

Frank was surprised at how heavy the creeper was. It was old, and the solid top looked like oak. The sides were bolted to two-by-twos every nine inches to reinforce the bottom. Its six wheels rolled as if they had just been oiled. He hated being under the car, but at least he wouldn't be on the ground. As he lay down and pushed himself underneath, he wondered how safe he was.

Maybe I should get under this smash-proof thing.

Frank heard footsteps on the gravel. The feet stopped, and Frank looked over to see polished oxfords peeking out from creased dress pants right next to the rear tire.

"Frank Woods! Is that you under that car?"

As soon as Frank saw the shoes, he knew it was Mr. Peterson; he didn't need the voice to confirm it. He would rather stay where he was.

"Yes, sir. Do you need me or my mother?"

"You, young man."

Frank didn't like the sound of that. He closed his eyes and squared his jaw. He didn't move.

"I've got to fix this oil leak, Mr. Peterson. My mama's inside, if you want to wait there. I'll come right in when I'm done."

"No, I'm not here for your mother. We already spoke."

Frank knew if Mr. Peterson had already spoken to his mother, then maybe he also knew about the bloody shirt and about the lockers.

Just then, a drop of oil leaked onto Frank's head and he remembered that he should be wearing those old goggles he had seen on the shelf. He turned his head so quickly that he slammed the wrench against the underbody, and it went flying. As he tried to catch it with his other hand, he smashed his thumb.

"Hey, Mr. Peterson, can you get that for me?"

Frank rolled over to the side of the car and stuck his hand out for the wrench.

"I guess you didn't take me seriously. I'm not here to help you fix a car."

As slowly as possible, Frank rolled himself out and sat up on the creeper.

"Frank, if I didn't know you better, I'd think you were hiding under there."

As he looked up at Mr. Peterson, he noticed how firmly he stood his ground—shoulders back, chest out, ready for action, despite his jacket and tie.

Why is he here? Can't everyone just leave me alone? But Frank knew he couldn't avoid this conversation any longer. He had ignored repeated opportunities to talk at school. The other day, when he had seen Mr. Peterson walking toward him in the hallway, he had ducked into the biology lab and gone through the storage room to get out the other side.

"Frank, I'm on my way to a meeting with Reverend Wilford and some others about some of the problems we've been seeing and hearing about. I haven't seen you at football practice. Why aren't you going?"

'Cause I can't play, so why practice? "Second string—why should I go?"

"Because you belong there, Frank. Are you going to let them push you out? You're making it too easy on them."

"*I'm* making it too easy on *them*? They're pushing and shoving too hard. It doesn't matter what I do. All the coaches want us to do is give them white boys a team to play against at practice."

Frank remembered the last tackle he had made. *The coach didn't hear, "Get off me, nigger—I'll take care of you later."*

Mr. Peterson just looked at him.

What do you know, standing there in your suit? Talk don't do no good. "We're as good as them, but they get to play on Saturdays."

"Boy, there is more to life than football."

For you, maybe. For my daddy, maybe. But not for me. I want out of this town. "Football and a scholarship are my way out of this place. Now it's not going to happen. I was counting on that scout coming to the Thanksgiving game to see me play. They won't let me play. I've been robbed."

Frank grabbed the wrench, lay back down, and rolled himself slowly back under the car. After a few minutes of silence, Mr. Peterson walked away. Frank drew in a deep breath and stayed on the creeper for a long time while he wished this man could help him.

Chapter 23

♥

Evelyn

Wednesday, November 26, 1969

Evelyn had never had a white woman as a friend, and she wasn't sure she wanted one. She sure didn't need *this* one. Tensions had run high since the closing of the black schools three weeks earlier, and Evelyn was in no mood to attract trouble.

Sure, Colleen seemed nice enough. She cared about her students and about Lulu, and she never gossiped or complained. But at times Evelyn found her unbelievably naive, and it kept falling on her shoulders to explain to this white woman how things worked down here.

As she walked toward the classroom trailer, Evelyn glanced around to ensure no one saw her. It was late, and Colleen's car sat alone in the side parking lot.

Colleen opened the trailer door just as Evelyn reached the steps. "Goodness, you startled me." Colleen pressed a hand to her chest. "I wish this door had a window. Did you need something? It's late and I was just leaving. Don't you need to get ready for Thanksgiving too?"

Evelyn gestured toward the inside of the trailer. She'd come to Colleen with a specific purpose in mind, and it was no conversation to have outside.

"Yes, but I need to talk to you."

"Of course. Come in." Colleen backed up and dropped her schoolbag.

Evelyn took a deep breath and sighed. "How was the library trip on Saturday?"

Colleen mumbled, "Fine, I guess. Two of the children weren't home when I went to get them."

Evelyn perched on the edge of a student's desk. "Yes, I know. Some folks are worried about you picking up the children. They're not used to white teachers coming to the house."

"But nobody had any reservations about the first two trips, and I checked with the families to remind them in advance. Why is there a problem this time? What changed?"

What changed? Our school closed.

Evelyn sighed. "I heard that a police officer stopped you at the top of the road. Is that so?"

"How do you know that?" Colleen asked slowly.

Evelyn nodded and waited for more.

"He asked if I was lost."

"Did he ask anything else?"

Colleen's pale cheeks flushed. "Well, he asked why a white woman would be driving down that road."

Evelyn felt her face tighten. *So it's true what Ole Man Everett heard.*

"Evelyn, what's wrong?"

Evelyn let out a bitter laugh, regretting that she'd promised Annie Mae she would have this conversation.

"Didn't you meet Cynthia's grandfather? Why do you think he watches those grandkids of his like a hawk? Haven't you heard of the Klan?"

Understanding seemed to dawn in Colleen's expression, but she didn't say anything. Finally, she shook her head. "What does that have to do with me?"

"There's a rumor spreading," Evelyn said. "Ole Man Everett saw your car get stopped by the police car that always patrols his neighborhood. He followed you on foot through the woods because the patrol car left just before you brought the children back. He was close enough to hear. Voices carry through those trees. Rumors are that you're registering black folks to vote."

"That doesn't make sense." Colleen shook her head.

"Colleen, it doesn't have to make sense. White people down here can be nasty and mean. It's just the way it is."

Evelyn paused, looking at Colleen's confused face. "Miz Woods asked me to tell you what's being said about you."

"Is that why she didn't send Rachel on Saturday?"

"Yes. The rumors started before you got pulled over. He's been looking out for you, that officer, Beau Harper." Evelyn leaned hard on the word *officer*.

"How would he know that I was taking my students to the library?"

"His wife is Rita Harper. She told him you were getting signatures."

"Rita? You mean that teacher with the perfect makeup? The one who pretends I don't exist? Yes, I'm getting signatures. For library cards." Colleen's hands balled into fists. "I'm touched that you and Miz Woods are concerned, Evelyn. But I can take care of myself."

Evelyn wanted nothing more than to be finished with this conversation, but somehow she had to make Colleen understand. "I think you don't know how things are around here. Miz Annie Mae realizes you only want to be kind to the children in your class. But kindness sets up some terrible things for us black folks."

"To be kind? All I'm trying to do is a good job."

Evelyn realized she had no choice but to be blunt. "You're putting our children in danger by taking them to the library." She spoke low, so her voice wouldn't travel beyond the trailer walls.

"Is that what you think?" Colleen replied, with a worried look.

"I have to go. I've already said too much, and I can't let anyone see me talking to you."

Evelyn left the trailer, treading lightly on the stairs so they wouldn't squeak.

Chapter 24

●

Colleen

Wednesday, November 26, 1969

The news shook Colleen to her core. She stared at the door for a long time after it closed gently.

Evelyn was right. She *didn't* know how things worked around here. It wasn't at all like *The Little Rascals*. She'd grown up watching the TV show, featuring Farina, Stymie, Buckwheat, and Alfalfa, poor black and white neighborhood friends whose adventures would have made any adult pull their own hair. No candles for the birthday cake? Use a firecracker. They had the He-Man Woman Haters Club and the Cluck Cluck Klams Club. That last one required meeting while wearing long white robes.

But the KKK wasn't a TV show, or a game, or a club. Colleen had never realized that the hatred ran so deep. It was more than signs like WHITES ONLY. Everyone else seemed to know the unwritten rules. She had tried to put on a brave front so Evelyn wouldn't think she was afraid. It had crossed her mind that she might be making herself a target, especially after the police officer had stopped her. Of course it had scared her, but she hadn't considered that she might be putting children in danger.

As she drove home, she struggled with her next steps. Ask Miguel? Of course he would say she shouldn't take the children to the library anymore. Confide in her father? Both men would want to protect her by eliminating the trip and therefore the danger. Was it smart or cowardly to stop?

Trust your gut. Take the warning, Colleen.

This felt like the time she'd had a research paper for her sociology class in college. The professor had been intrigued by the topic. Colleen had planned to interview local realtors. The research question had been "What is the basis of the demographic profile of the residents in her hometown?"

She remembered how confident she felt as she pulled up to the first realty office. That morning she wore her teacher interview clothes, a gray-and-white pin-striped gabardine suit. She had visited the library and found the census reports of the three towns bordering hers. She had the demographic information and statistics ready to back up her questions. A clipboard neatly held the questionnaires she had prepared.

Her view of her town as full of kind and reasonable people was clouded by the fact that not one black individual lived in it. The most common black faces she saw there belonged to men hopping on and off the garbage trucks as they drove down the streets and the one Negro cashier at the town's supermarket, where she worked part-time. He went to a local college like she did. He also brought in the carts from the parking lot and unloaded the trucks in the back of the store.

The birds chirped on that bright, sunny April day as she walked up the landscaped concrete walk to the front door. There were four doorbells. Colleen pressed the one for Hometown Realty. A middle-aged woman wearing a shirtwaist dress buttoned up tight opened the door. Her dark red lipstick appeared freshly applied, and Colleen noticed a spot on her teeth when she smiled.

"Good morning. We're just opening. Do you have an appointment?"

Colleen shifted the clipboard when she noticed the woman's eyes drift to it.

"No, I'm a student at Teachers College, and I'm taking a survey. Are you the realtor?"

"No, I'm a secretary. Why don't you come in, and I'll ask the owner to speak to you?"

Colleen waited in the center of the office and tried to appear professional. The secretary hurried into an adjacent room. After a few minutes, a man came out to speak to her.

"Well, young lady, I understand that you have some questions for a school project?"

"Not a school project, but a survey that's part of a research paper for one of my college classes. It won't take very long. I'll just ask a few questions and take some notes."

"What is the topic?"

Colleen wished he would ask her to sit so that she could take notes. Her purse kept slipping off her shoulder when she held the clipboard to write on it.

"It's a study of the community as an example of suburban life, which appears to exclude Negroes, when compared with adjoining communities."

The realtor turned to speak with the secretary, who was now seated at a desk. The secretary's eyes widened as he asked, "What is my appointment schedule this morning?"

She flipped through the calendar and answered, "You're booked till three."

Colleen looked around. No one else was there.

"I'm sorry, but I really don't have time. Perhaps you can give me the questionnaire and come back later?"

She had no choice if she wanted the survey answered.

Colleen shook his hand with a firm grip as she handed him the questionnaire. The realtor adjusted his glasses and shook his head as he glanced at it.

By the time she walked up the path to the third realty office, she knew that word had spread. A kindly gentleman met her at the door and suggested that she could get all of her questions answered if she went to see the person whose name and address were written on the index card he held out for her. She recognized the address. It was a Protestant church near her home.

As she recalled the meeting with the minister, Colleen could still feel his resistance cloaked in sincerity. He wanted to know if she was having trouble at home, if she worked with a group, if other students had surveyed the other towns. He didn't answer any of the survey's questions. None of the realtors did either.

Then Colleen remembered the reason the black cashier had quit working at the supermarket. It was after the second time he'd been stopped by police, who had demanded to know why he'd been driving through town after dark, going home from the job. Now, in a curious reversal, it was her turn: stopped because a white woman shouldn't be driving through the black section of town. The black cashier had quit with the comment "This isn't the mountain I want to die on."

Remembering his statement helped her to decide. The risk was real and involved more than her. She wouldn't take the children to the library anymore.

Chapter 25

🍎

Evelyn

Wednesday, November 26, 1969

After Evelyn delivered Annie Mae's message to Colleen, she worried that someone would see her leaving. It was almost five o'clock, and in the short days of November, the setting sun cast shadows that made her nervous. She walked around to the front of the school, where her car was parked. A light from inside the main office fanned out shards of light like a flashlight in the dark.

It must be Mr. Peterson. Just like at West Hill.

She considered stopping in to talk to him, like she'd enjoyed doing in the past. But she couldn't shake the feeling that someone was watching from inside the school. Maybe the light wasn't from Peterson's office. Maybe it wasn't he; after all, it was a shared space.

Nothing was the same.

When she was seated in her car, she leaned back, breathing in the cool air of the late-fall day. She hurried home, worrying the whole way.

A knock on the back door interrupted Evelyn as she pre-pared her supper. The key to open the dead bolt was on a hook hidden by the gingham curtains. Evelyn lived alone at the end of a quiet street. She didn't get many uninvited visitors in the evening, and fewer still at the back door. After school, the children sometimes played in the wooded fields near her small house but they never crossed through the fencing that protected her garden or through the gate to the back of the house.

Evelyn switched on the light over the stoop. She was relieved to see Annie Mae Woods holding a basket covered with a red-and-white-checked cloth. A stained apron over her housedress was a surprise. It was unusual to see her friend look unkempt.

Evelyn released the dead bolt and then the latch to the screen door and invited Annie Mae inside.

"I could smell those famous biscuits of yours right through this door. How is one person going to eat all of them? Come in, come in."

As she stepped over the threshold, Evelyn heard a sigh as Annie Mae handed the basket to her. "These are some extras I made for our Thanksgiving dinner. I saw you as you drove past my house; it's after dark tonight. You had a long day. It's late to be fixing a meal—thought you could use something easy. I'm guessing you spoke to Miz Rodriguez, like I asked."

"My, my, but you don't give yourself a chance to rest, Annie Mae. Yes, I told her. No need to worry about me, but I do appreciate the company tonight."

"Frank is home, helping Rachel with some homework, and Sissy is playing with Baby James. It seemed like a good time to talk a bit, if you don't mind."

"Sit yourself down, now; we can talk over tea and biscuits while I finish warming up this chicken stew from yesterday. I have plenty. Do you want some?"

□□

"Just some tea, thank you."

Evelyn took out her favorite teapot, the china one with the purple-and-green wisteria painted over the bone-white background. Aunt Dorothy had given it to her when she'd graduated from college. Evelyn smiled as she lifted it up and noticed the blue imprint on the base. It had a ribbon with a crown over the name of the manufacturer: SADLER—MADE IN ENGLAND. She was convinced that the tea brewed in that pot tasted the best. Evelyn was pleased to be able to use the matching cups, saucers, and dessert plates for her company. They didn't really match, and they weren't made in England, but she pretended they were.

The teapot reminded Evelyn of her aunt's courage. Sometimes she thought if she drank enough tea from that pot, it would give her the fortitude she wished she had. Her aunt and uncle had met at Hampton Institute in Virginia. Aunt Dorothy had been the first of her mother's sisters to go to away to college at a time when it was difficult for any woman, especially a Negro woman, to be allowed to live away from home. Her family believed in schools for Negroes. Education was foremost, not integration. Her uncle believed in both. Aunt Dorothy tried to convince her Virginian husband to come back with her to Louisiana, but he had his sights set on setting up a restaurant in Houston with some of his classmates, and that was what they did. She became a teacher, and he was a businessman. They were part of a group of educated and successful Negroes. The group pressured the businesses in their community to accept integration, and those that didn't were faced with scornful stories and photos from Negro writers and photographers. Her aunt then led the group to work with some determined white librarians to quietly desegregate the Houston Public Library in 1953.

Evelyn thought back to the day *her* library opened.

□□□

They put the chairs on the lawn.

"Evelyn, you haven't said a word to me since you asked me if I wanted to eat some chicken stew."

"Oh, I'm sorry. This library thing with Colleen has me thinking of my aunt."

"What does your aunt have to do with it?"

"Annie Mae, you know how some white folks were thinking that Miz Rodriguez was getting signatures? They don't care if she's helping us get library cards or signing us up to vote—it's all the same to that kind in this town."

Evelyn checked the color of the steeped tea and poured the first cup for Annie Mae. She laid a biscuit drizzled with honey on the plate and gave her friend a lace-trimmed cloth napkin.

"Don't you remember what happened the day our library opened, Annie Mae? It wasn't that long ago . . . Well, maybe it's been ten years, but it seems like yesterday to me."

"Ten years ago, I had three youngins—Frank was eight, Sissy was four, and Rachel was just born—and no time to care about a library being built."

"Those uppity white women you iron for took the chairs out of the library so that we couldn't sit at the tables. They had a read-in."

"A read-in?"

"Yes, like the ones in Alabama. I just wanted to have a good library and some new books. But they were so worried about their books, they didn't want us to come inside. I heard one of them say they didn't want to touch a book that a colored hand had touched."

Or sit on a chair still warm from me.

"Who said that?"

"The same one causing trouble for Colleen, Rita Harper. The one with that cop husband. He was the one who stopped her."

"I don't iron for her."

"No, but you work for her friends, and they sure stick together, don't they?"

Evelyn realized that Annie Mae wasn't paying much attention to her. Of course she knew what a read-in and a sit-in and even a freedom ride were. Something else must be wrong. Her face was drawn, her eyes were clouded, and Annie Mae looked like she had when the sorrow of losing her husband had almost taken her.

"Annie Mae, what's wrong? I know you were worried about Rachel and your nephew Jarrod going to the library, but I told Colleen why you aren't going to send them, so we just have to wait and see what she does. It's up to her."

"No, it's not that—it's Frank."

Evelyn knew how much Annie Mae counted on Frank since he was now the man of the family. She lifted the teapot to pour them both another cup of fortitude.

"Tell me. It's my turn to listen to you."

"He's getting into trouble. Came home with a bloody shirt stashed inside his bag. Didn't want me to see it. He won't tell me what happened."

"But you talked with Mr. Peterson after they walked out of the school. Wouldn't he call you in?"

"No, I don't think it happened at school. I don't know what to do. He's been wandering around after school, letting me think he was at practice. When I found the bloody shirt, he got angry and told me that he gave up football practice since he can't play. He hates being second string. He's upset because he can't play in the Thanksgiving game tomorrow."

Evelyn reached over and placed her hand on Annie Mae's. Nothing was the same.

Chapter 26

◉

Colleen

Thursday, February 5, 1970

"I missed you so much at Christmas, my heart aches. I'm all thumbs this morning. Oh yeah—it's Saturday, January thirty-first. This will be quick. I have to get this tape to the post office today. So let me pretend that it's February fifth.

"Happy birthday, Colleen! Hope you are enjoying a warm and, of course, snow-free day. It's been so cold here. The wind makes it feel like below zero. Please send me more news about your students. I expect that you have everything under control by now. It's hard to believe that I had to send your posters and the wall alphabet. Why can't they get those for you? I'm glad to help—you know that. Anything else? I love you. Signing off. Dad."

Colleen shut off the tape player, knowing she would play the message again later to relish the sound of his voice. The cassette had arrived just on time. It was the second kindness of the day, but neither one lifted her spirits for more than a moment. She put the tape player away. What could she tell him? Today she was frayed around the edges. If anyone pulled the thread, she would unravel.

Her eyes drifted over to the counter. Now, that was a real surprise—a cake. Colleen had saved the last piece of birthday cake for Miguel. She recalled the confusion when she opened the classroom trailer door as she and her students had returned from lunch.

"Miz Rodriguez, look. There's a cake on your desk. A big cake!" Linkston shouted.

As she tried to understand what he was telling her, the children all rushed past her and squeezed around her desk. She froze when she saw Cynthia lift a large knife.

"Cynthia! Stop!"

Cynthia turned with the knife still in her hands. "It's to cut the cake, Miz Rodriguez."

"Children, please! Sit at your desks."

"Let me see . . . What is this?"

"Cynthia, put the knife *down.*"

Colleen saw Cynthia's chin tremble and her eyes fill up as she set the knife on the desk.

"I was trying to help, Miz Rodriguez."

"Why is there a cake on your desk?" Jarrod asked.

"Children, children, you must sit *down.*"

"*Cake?* Can we have a piece?"

"Do you have ice cream?"

Only a few students had listened to her. She couldn't get near the desk because they filled the narrow rows. She was beyond frustration; it was stuffy in the trailer, and she couldn't reach the air conditioner. It would circulate some air, and the drone would muffle the commotion.

"If you are not in your seats by the time I count to three . . ."

What? Colleen, what? What will you do?

"One . . . two . . . three."

Most of the children scattered and sat down, but Jarrod still hovered near her desk, looking at the cake.

Is he licking his finger?

"Jarrod! God d . . . bless America."

I almost said damn. *For crying out loud, calm yourself, Colleen.*

Colleen watched as Jarrod finally moved to take his seat. She couldn't understand what had just happened. Chaos? Over a cake? On her birthday? Who could have done this? She hadn't told anyone, as far as she could remember.

As the children moved away, she was finally able to stand behind her desk. Four rows of faces stared back at her. Then she looked at the cake. It was amazing. It appeared to be at least three layers and bigger than a dinner plate. The icing was in fluffy yellow peaks, spaced neatly around the circumference. The "knife" wasn't a knife, at least not a sharp one, as it had appeared from the other side of the room. It was a pointed cake server with a china handle. A pile of napkins lay next to a note.

"Happy birthday, Colleen, from Evelyn."

Evelyn?

At least the children had stopped clamoring. What should she do now? Thirty pairs of eager eyes gave her the answer.

She cut the cake and served it on the napkins. The afternoon was lost. She read them books and let them color on the special manuscript lined paper that she had finally managed to get from the stockroom.

Her father thought she had everything under control. Evelyn had made her a cake. It was all too much to take in. The cake was to have been a treat, but it had only made the students harder to manage. Her father's message should have cheered her, but all the confidence she'd had back in August had disappeared.

Thirty children came to her every day with hope on their faces. But the pride they'd had in their classroom back at West

Hill School was fading as well. Winter in Louisiana meant that they wore light sweaters or maybe jackets. There was no place to keep those garments except on the backs of their chairs. When they pushed in their chairs for reading group, a sweater sometimes fell off and then someone stepped on it. Or it got stuck on the desk because the space was too tight, and they cried that their mama would be mad if it ripped.

The cramped space, the lack of materials, and five hours inside an air-conditioned trailer without windows was challenging, to say the least. Not being able to use the library trips as an incentive exhausted Colleen's spirit further.

So, give them a piece of cake, let them color away the afternoon. Did it matter? Did anything she was doing matter? Three months in this box already, four more to go. She wondered how she would last.

The next morning, Colleen went directly to Evelyn's classroom to return the plate and cake server. Evelyn was at the blackboard, which was on the long side of the classroom trailer, instead of on the short side, where Colleen's was positioned. The room was arranged with the desks in a way that made the space appear more open. Evelyn also had her desk behind the students, not in front like Colleen did. Maybe she should change her layout too. Would it help? It couldn't be worse.

Colleen saw Evelyn smile as she walked toward her.

First the cake; now what?

"Evelyn, thank you. The cake was delicious, and the children really enjoyed it. But how did you know it was my birthday?"

"You told me. Remember the Sunshine Club we had back at West Hill School?"

Colleen put the plate and server down on Evelyn's desk. "Yes, of course, but I didn't realize we were doing it here at Kettle Creek."

Evelyn placed the cake items in a bag under her desk and looked directly into Colleen's eyes. "We're not. I am."

Colleen thought about some of the teachers in Kettle Creek's lunchroom. They wouldn't have eaten a cake baked by a Negro. Well, they would have if it were their maid, using their pans and utensils, in their house. What a coincidence that Evelyn had baked her favorite: a lemon-flavored cake with creamy lemon icing, just like her mother would've made.

Chapter 27

*

Colleen

Monday, February 9, 1970

When the children got to school the following Monday, they had a surprise. Linkston was always the first to arrive, much earlier than everyone else. He used to stand on the 2C line outside by the tree, until one rainy day Colleen invited him in to wait. From that day on, he always opened the door to the trailer, looking for Mrs. Rodriguez. She was always at her desk, right by the door.

"Miz Rodriguez! What are you doing way back there?" he asked today.

Colleen had placed her desk right under the air conditioner in the back of the room. She reasoned that it was better there because she rarely sat at it, and she gained a few feet by pushing it back into the corner. The previous Friday afternoon, she had rearranged the student desks and the reading center and had created a bulletin board on the long side of the room.

"Where's my desk, Miz Rodriguez? The classroom is upside down!"

Colleen laughed and stood to show Linkston his new place.

She had placed the desks in five clusters of six, with three desks facing three others. She had created "tables" like the ones she had used in New Jersey.

"Look, Linkston, everyone's name is on their desk. When the children come in today, can you help me?"

"Yes, ma'am! I can read everyone's name!" He adjusted his glasses as he walked around the desks to read the bright yellow index card attached to each one. He stood up just a bit taller and straighter. Or had he grown? His big smile lit up his eyes and revealed some missing teeth. She hadn't seen that smile in some time. Linkston was always so serious. The transition had hit him harder than the others. He and Cynthia had been the last ones to go on a Saturday library trip.

"Let's go meet the class, Linkston. It's time."

As Colleen walked toward her post, she saw the lines of children waiting for their teachers. Four lines were all Negroes. Why did they call this integration? It wasn't, not really. The lines for the other classes had all the white children at the front and the Negro children in line behind them. Was it better or worse for the black children in the "integrated" classrooms? At least her children weren't treated like second-class citizens.

As usual, Cynthia claimed the first position, with Jarrod right behind her, nudging her to move as soon as Colleen appeared. Cynthia stood her ground. Colleen knew that the child never wanted to disappoint her teacher.

"Good morning, chickadees!" As Colleen greeted her class, she did a quick head count. "Looks like everyone's here. Okay, Cynthia, lead the class. I have a surprise for all of you."

Colleen and Linkston helped the students find their new places. When the children were set, Colleen realized she would need to go over some rules.

Questions peppered the air: "Why do I have to sit next to her?"

And then complaints: "My mama says not to talk to him."

"Children, let's try it out. Which table is ready? Who can get their math work out first?"

Praising the children, table by table, for pulling out their books, pencils, and rulers worked to stop the chatter and begin the day. The change would take time and patience. Now the children didn't have to pass their chairs through the narrow aisles because Colleen had placed them by their reading groups and would take her chair to them.

But by lunchtime, she questioned the rearrangement of the desks. The students never left their seats for the entire morning. The new desk placement caused a lot of snickering and face making that she hadn't anticipated. The children were used to looking at the back of someone's head, not at one other. The narrow rows were gone. They had served as a place for the students to line up so that she could take them to lunch in the expected orderly manner.

"Stand up and push in your chairs. I'll call one table at a time to line up by the door."

The first twelve students assembled across the back of the room. Colleen could see that that wasn't going to work because they crowded into the space. After sitting all morning, the children were bursting with energy.

Just get them outside!

Walking to the lunchroom with the sun warming their heads and shoulders calmed them. Colleen was relieved to deliver them to the lunch aides. She needed to be out of that tin-can classroom as much as her students did.

The afternoon was worse. Colleen tried everything. She had them stand in their places and play Simon Says, she let them march around the room to play Follow the Leader, and she praised them. Nothing worked. Then she remembered what Evelyn had told her back at West Hill months earlier: "Did you see the black strap in your middle drawer?"

Colleen remembered her surprise when she'd realized that the thick black belt was in her desk for a purpose.

"You better use it from time to time; otherwise, they won't respect you, and they'll get the upper hand."

Colleen had promised herself that she would never use the belt. How could she hit a child with it? It was two or three inches wide, soft and flexible, and could encircle her waist almost twice. Every time she opened the drawer, she could smell the leather. It was a good smell, like new shoes, but it provoked some terrible thoughts: images from TV news, white faces full of rage, angry racist chants.

A ruckus from the back of the room drew her out of the memory.

"Jarrod. Sit down."

He was still unhappy about losing Simon Says, and he had grabbed Linkston's glasses. The two boys were struggling.

"Give me my glasses back. Don't break them."

Colleen rushed over and reached between them to get the glasses.

"Jarrod. Stop."

Colleen saw a look she didn't recognize from Jarrod. He clenched his teeth and squeezed his eyes tightly, then pulled away from her. Linkston looked ready to cry, Jarrod ready to run.

Colleen rushed to her desk and opened the drawer. The smell of leather wafted up like a warning.

"Jarrod, come here."

His anger turned to fear as he dragged himself to her desk.

He knew what was in that drawer. She remembered him asking if she would use it when they were still at West Hill School.

Colleen took out the belt and hit the desk with a *whack* that echoed in the trailer.

"Do you want me to hit you?" She heard her words as if someone else had said them.

He shook his head from side to side so fast that some of the kids giggled.

"Then *sit down*." He did. So did she.

The rest of the afternoon was quiet, but it wasn't a good type of quiet. Shame filled her up. She had crossed the line. She couldn't control the circumstances that had put her in this tin-can classroom, but she must control her response.

Chapter 28

🍎

Colleen

Saturday, February 28, 1970

ebruary was Colleen's favorite month for two reasons: her
birthday and snow. At home in New Jersey, the cold, crisp
days and surprise snowstorms often meant a day or two off from
school. She could have used that this week. Miguel had been
impatient with her mood lately, and she couldn't blame him.
She didn't know how he managed to be the tough drill sergeant
all day yet leave that personality back in the barracks every
evening. Her birthday was over. The classroom was a disaster.
She was miserable. And where was he, anyway? It was Saturday and the last day of February.

"Colleen. Colleen!" She heard Miguel's shout over a rumbling noise that vibrated the metal walls of the trailer. She
threw open the trailer door to find him sitting on a motorcycle
with a helmet on his head and one in his hand.

"Get your jacket and hop on." He laughed as he revved the
engine.

Frozen in place, Colleen had to shout over the noise. "Where
did you get a motorcycle?"

"The supply sergeant lent it to me; we have it for the day. Are you coming or not?"

Colleen put on the helmet and sat behind Miguel. She had to hold on to him for dear life as he turned off the gravel road onto the paved highway, but the ride lifted Colleen's spirits, and soon she was laughing along with him. They turned off at a bend in the road that led to a backwoods creek. They stopped to sit on a rock ledge overlooking the gentle stream.

"This ride seems to have taken your mind off things. How 'bout I make some Texas hash for supper?"

"We can both do it," she replied, giving him a big grin and a bigger hug.

On the way back, they went through town and stopped at the Piggly Wiggly for a package of chopped meat and rice. He put the groceries in the saddlebag of the motorcycle. Colleen asked, "Can we make one more stop, at the five-and-dime? I need some nail polish remover."

"Not much room left," he said, as he fastened the buckle.

"It's small—don't worry. Wait here. I'll be quick," she replied.

The five-and-dime had old counters with items arranged in bins, not on shelves. At the end of the counter was a stack of children's coloring books that a clerk was putting into larger bins. Colleen took a look at them. Sometimes she found letter or number puzzles that she used for extra worksheets during reading group. She was surprised to find paperback cursive-writing books. Back home, children learned cursive in the spring of second grade. Kettle Creek Schools didn't have that practice, but no one seemed to be watching what she did, so why not? It would be a new thing to teach, to challenge them with. Something they could be proud of. She bought all the books, ten, not enough for all her students, but each book had several practice pages for every letter. They could share. She picked up thirty no. 2 pencils and paid for the purchase.

When she came out with a shopping bag from McCory's, Miguel had straddled the motorcycle and was ready to go. He shook his head. "What's this?"

Colleen laughed and placed the package between them. "I found something that will help me for next week."

"*Dios mío,*" he shouted over the rumbling of the engine. She reached around him and hugged him tighter so the books wouldn't fall.

On Monday, Colleen handed out the cursive-writing booklets. As she expected, the children were motivated to learn how to write like the older kids and their parents.

"Oh, my mama writes like this," Rachel said. "It's so pretty. Sissy, my sister, and even my brother, Frank, can write like this."

Colleen demonstrated writing the first letter on the chalkboard. "Who can tell me what letter this is?" Excited hands waved in the air. "Cynthia?"

"*C!*" she shouted. "It's my letter."

Colleen explained that they would learn the magic letters first. "They're called magic letters because they're almost like the printed versions, and *c* is the first one. Then comes *a*, and then *d*. Soon you'll be able to write words by connecting the letters. Let's practice."

Chapter 29

♠

Frank

Thursday, March 5, 1970

Frank heard the phone ring when his mother was in the kitchen, drying the last of the supper dishes.

"Frank, Dedra's on the phone." His mother smiled and handed the phone to him. He knew she liked Dedra. "That girl has spunk," she used to say. But that had been when Dedra was the cheerleading captain at West Hill High. When she had cheered for him.

He took the phone into the pantry behind the kitchen and closed the door. He missed talking to Dedra. It was hard to see her since he had stopped going to football practice. He used to walk her home afterward and had planned to ask her to the senior prom. But that was at West Hill. Would there even be a prom now?

"Frank, why didn't you come meet us at the tennis courts? We need everyone to help plan and organize for the walkout."

The tennis courts.

He sat on the floor in the dark. Did she care about him, or was he just another body in her protest now?

Frank remembered the first time he had kissed her, after one of her solo tennis practices the previous fall. They hadn't had tennis rackets, but they had tossed a ball back and forth. Dedra had told him about Althea Gibson and how Althea had shaken hands with Queen Elizabeth after winning Wimbledon. He could still hear her hope when she'd said, "Maybe I can meet Althea someday. Or Rosa Parks."

He lost himself, thinking about her and listening to her breathing in his ear.

"Frank?"

He hadn't gone to the tennis courts. He didn't want to call attention to himself. The last time he had joined a walkout, he'd gotten arrested. He needed time to think this over.

"Well, we're walking out at noon. I wanted you to know."

He heard an angry edge to her voice. He still didn't answer. He wanted to hear her soft breathing.

"Frank?" She stopped speaking.

Her silence worried him.

"I couldn't go to the planning meeting. My mama needed me to watch Rachel and Baby James."

The lie was too transparent.

"Don't you want to see me? Why couldn't Sissy have watched them? She's old enough."

He couldn't explain why he hadn't gone. He was trying to figure it out himself."Frank, what's wrong with you?"

He admired Dedra. She was ready to fight for all the players and all the cheerleaders and all the black students. He wasn't like her: his disappointment over not playing football cut too deep, and he was having trouble fighting for himself.

"Frank, we don't have any senior privileges. We've got three more months of senior year. We at least want our prom. And what about next year? We don't have our spots on the student council, even though I was president at West Hill. You couldn't play football. We're going to sit on the lawn until we get representation. Will you be there?"

"I'll think about it, Dedra."

"We need to do more than think. The principal promised us he would set it up, but it never happened."

Frank remembered the meeting in the main office with his mother and Mr. Peterson the day after the first walkout. The office had been available because Mr. Armstrong had met with some of the West Hill students that day. That was when promises had been made. But now months had passed, and there still wasn't any representation for the black students in any sports or student government at Kettle Creek High School. His football teammates and the cheerleaders had organized a second walkout. And Dedra was their leader. It didn't matter that it wasn't official.

Frank remembered the quiet girl he'd met when they were freshmen. *She's not quiet anymore. She wants to be like Rosa Parks and Althea Gibson.*

The next day during his fourth-period class, Frank kept looking at the clock. At noon, he held his breath. Chairs scraped the floor. Footsteps followed. His English teacher turned from the board as the door opened. Five or six Negro students lined up quietly to walk out of the room. Frank saw his teacher, Dr. Willa Henson, frown at what was happening. She pushed her glasses above her forehead to get her blond hair out of her eyes. Then two of the girls left the line and went over to her, saying, "We want to leave, Dr. Henson."

"But why? What will this accomplish?"

"We need to be heard."

Frank was surprised to hear his teacher tell them, "I know. Go ahead."

He looked around to see the remaining students, all white, just sitting and waiting for what would happen next.

Frank stood up and walked to the window. He looked down at the lawn in the front of the building. From his third-floor view, he could see the street and the circular drive around the flagpole. Black students stopped to take brown bags from parents who seemed to have known this was going to happen and were actually making deliveries. Laughter echoed up to him as the students sat on the grass and began to eat their lunch as if they were at a picnic—except for Dedra. He saw her stand to speak to the principal. He knew what the request was. He wondered what the answer would be.

If the principal and the coaches could be like Dr. Henson, things might be better. Frank had been selected for this class. It was a small class of sixteen students, chosen for their potential and maturity. Today they were writing in their journals after having a discussion about the crossover and the challenge black and white students were having about the attitude "This is the way we do things, and this is the way we don't."

He had never had a teacher who was called Doctor. She expected more of Frank than any teacher ever had. Not just neat and nicely written pages—she wanted his thoughts.

His heart was racing; he had made up his mind. He sat back down at his desk.

More students were leaving their classrooms, shouting and slamming doors.

As he sat in his chair, his teacher sat on the edge of her desk. She looked at him for a long time before she spoke.

"Frank, you were on the football team, weren't you? I heard you were a star player at West Hill."

"Yes, ma'am. I was."

"Well, don't you want to be heard too?"

"Yes, ma'am, but I'm not going to miss class. I'm going to graduate, and I'm going to college."

Dr. Henson studied him. She ignored the white kids, who were whispering and shaking their heads. Then she said, "Well, there's more than one way to succeed at something. All right, class. Let's continue our discussion."

Chapter 30

🍎

Colleen

Friday, March 20, 1970

olleen walked to Evelyn's classroom trailer to bring some of the carpet squares she had managed to get from the local Carpets My Way. Colleen had had the idea of asking for out-of- date samples so she could take the children outside to sit on the lawn behind the trailer. The manager had been kind and given her enough for her class, plus ten more.

"I can't believe you got anyone to give you these," Evelyn said, as she opened the door.

"It all happened after a stop at the library. That young librarian who's been collecting books for me to use with my class told me where the shop was. You know, Jeanne, the one with the braces."

Evelyn shook her head. "No, I don't go to that library."

Colleen handed her the carpet pieces with raised eyebrows. "Why not, Evelyn?"

Evelyn took the pieces and turned to put them down. "My concern, not yours. Leave it at that."

Colleen sat on a student desk and plowed on, ignoring the

gaffe. "Oh, right, well, I told Jeanne that I had some carpet samples in my classroom last year for story-time sit-upons. She was the one who recommended I speak to her friend who manages the shop."

Evelyn didn't seem to be listening as she piled the sit-upons on a student's chair.

"I never would have found the shop if she hadn't explained exactly where it was, at the end of Main Street, tucked back near the railroad crossing. I told her friend that Jeanne sent me and that I was a second-grade teacher at Kettle Creek Elementary School. He couldn't have been nicer."

Evelyn stood back to look at the stack of carpets she had piled on the small seat. "I'll find a better spot to store them when we get back from spring break. Where did you put yours?"

"For now, they're under the spare desk I use to set up the library books." Colleen cleared her throat and waited for Evelyn to face her, then said, "I want to thank you for listening to me after that disaster with Jarrod. Your idea to take the children out of the trailer for some of our lessons has made all the difference. We're happier outside. And the carpet squares help them stay in one spot."

"I'm glad it worked out. Thank you for the bringing me these. I never would have thought of using them."

The stack of sit-upons tilted and landed on the floor. "Some of these are big enough for two kids to sit on—that's why they fell," Evelyn said. She restacked them and left them on the floor. She took her sweater from the back of the chair, folded it over her arm, and picked up her pocketbook. "Sorry, don't mean to rush you out, but I have to get home. I'm traveling to Baton Rouge as soon as I pack up my suitcase."

Colleen stood to leave. "That sounds nice. Let's get out of here, then. Miguel doesn't have the week off, but I sure can use it."

Colleen thought about how different Evelyn had become since their mentor meetings back at West Hill. Things had changed right before Christmas, when she'd warned Colleen that the Klan was watching her take the children to the library. Then Evelyn had remembered her birthday with a cake. Now they actually shared ideas. It was nice. She felt like they were true friends as they walked to the parking lot together.

Chapter 31

🍎

Evelyn

Friday, March 20, 1970

The pounding on her front door startled Evelyn. As she rushed down the stairs, she heard someone shout, "Miz Glover! Are you home?"

The frosted glass window couldn't hide the young man's bulk.

She opened it and said, "What's wrong, Frank? Does your mama need me?"

His fist was still raised from banging on the door. Evelyn saw his mouth shift from a hard line into a lopsided grin.

"I didn't mean to startle you. I wanted to ask you a question." He looked directly into her eyes with a confidence she hadn't seen before.

"Come in, let's sit in the parlor. I'm in a hurry, but we can talk for a bit. I'm leaving soon to visit some friends."

Frank sat on the edge of a side chair. He leaned forward with his hands on his knees. She clearly recalled how they had both lost their fathers in the same year. Frank's father's funeral service was the last one her father had planned before his massive heart attack.

"Go on, ask me."

"When you sold your parents' funeral business and bought this house, I helped out for a while. Do you remember?" Frank asked.

"Of course I remember that. I think you helped move the very chair you're sitting in."

He looked around the room and studied the furniture, piece by piece, before he spoke again. "Yes, ma'am, I did, and back then you said if I ever needed help, I could come to you."

"If I can help you, I will. What do you need?"

The last she had heard from his mother was that he wasn't seeing his friends, had stopped going to church, and spent a lot of time in his room.

He took a deep breath and explained, "I need a job to save up for college. I saw an ad from Glover Funeral Services in the paper. Mr. Fields, the new owner, is looking for help. I can work after school and on weekends. I wanted to ask you to put in a good word for me."

She considered the request. Evelyn had never wanted to become an undertaker. Her father's death had given her a way out. Frank's interest in working there surprised her.

"Of course I will, but all you have to do is go over and apply in person. Use my name as a reference. Remind them that you helped me move out of the apartment above the funeral rooms."

As she walked him to the door he had almost banged open a short time earlier, she thought of how proud his father would be. Frank would find a way to go to college, even without a football scholarship. She went upstairs to finish packing.

Evelyn felt the tension in her body release as she sank into the driver's seat. The trip to Baton Rouge would give her a lot of time to think, as well as a chance to breathe deeply and exhale with laughter, something she sorely needed. Lavinia would take her back to a time she had been freer, before her parents had died. Before everything had changed in the schools.

Evelyn parked the car in front of a familiar house and leaned back to listen to the subtle sound of the swelling Mississippi River rushing past on its way to the watershed basin below. Excited shouts pierced the river sounds.

"You're here! How wonderful to see you!" Lavinia cried, as she ran to open the car door.

"You look younger every time I see you. And you've straightened your hair. I like it," Evelyn said.

"I always admired your smooth style, and I'm not ready for an Afro yet."

Right behind Lavinia was her husband, and behind him were two children whom Evelyn didn't recognize. They'd been babies the last time she'd seen them.

"Come. Remember the twins? Look at my boys." Lavinia glanced over her shoulder with pride.

Two indistinguishable faces peeked out from behind her. Both had dimples and close-cut hair revealing perfectly shaped heads.

"I can't believe how they've grown. It's been too long. Which is Martin, and which is Gregory?"

Lavinia guided her boys toward Evelyn. "Show your manners, sons."

As the two boys extended their small hands, Evelyn felt pangs of envy, but she managed to keep it hidden.

Lavinia touched them on their heads. "They're in the advanced second-grade class and were just accepted into our church's boys' choir."

"But who is who?"

"I'm Martin, and he's Gregory," Martin said, as he pointed to his identically dressed brother.

"Sorry, but I'll need more help than that," Evelyn said, laughing.

The two women exchanged smiles as the boys' patience for manners erupted into pokes and giggles.

"Let's go inside and settle you into your room," Lavinia said.

Each boy took up a small case as they followed their father, who carried Evelyn's large bag. Evelyn carried a bulky brown paper carton that the curious boys kept peeking at. She responded to their unasked questions with a wink and a finger to her lips as she whispered, "Later."

"Thank you, Martin, Gregory. Daddy will take you to choir practice while Auntie Evelyn and I catch up." Lavinia ushered her sons out the door.

Evelyn had lived with Lavinia's family when the two of them attended Southern. Lavinia and her husband owned the house now and had turned the bedroom into a guest room. "I always loved this room," Evelyn said, "and I was thrilled to share it with you."

Lavinia rolled her eyes as she sat on the bed. "Remember how we used to have to close the door so my annoying little sisters wouldn't badger us with their silliness?"

Evelyn was the only child of elderly parents. Lavinia was the eldest of five. Evelyn's parents had agreed that she could live away at college if she'd stay with their friends. She had been grateful to find a companion her own age.

"I remember the long nights when we would lie awake, talking and confessing about stolen kisses. Who was that first love of yours, Lavinia?"

Laughter rose just as Evelyn realized who it was. She

clapped a hand over her mouth. "Gregory! You named your son after your first boyfriend? Why didn't I ever put that together?"

"This room will never give away our secrets, and neither will you, if you know what's good for you."

Evelyn knew what was good for her. It was good being here with her dear friend. She felt months of pent-up tension leave her as she delighted in the easy exchange.

"What are you telling me? Do you still have a sweet spot for him? Who was Martin named for? I don't remember a Martin."

The two women laughed at memories until the twins returned, running up the stairs and into the room.

Evelyn handed them the gift she had brought from Kettle Creek. Lavinia was as astonished as the twins when they tore off the wrapping of the large package to see an *Apollo* moon rocket model kit.

"How did you get this? Look, boys, the rocket has three stages and a lunar module," Lavinia said, as she read from the side of the box.

Squeals of excitement reached the living room, and Lawrence came up to see what was happening. Evelyn explained that a friend had purchased the kit at the army base's post exchange. After the moon landing the prior summer, the base had stocked a large shipment of the kits.

"They're interested in the space race and the moon landing, aren't they?" Evelyn asked.

Lavinia answered her with a hug that took her breath away and said, "You've been too busy since your mama and then your papa passed. You need to visit us more often."

"This is very special, sons. Let's take it to your room and put it together after we eat our dinner," Lawrence said.

After dinner and the rocket assembly, Martin and Gregory asked if Auntie Evelyn could read them a story before bedtime.

Evelyn felt her heart flutter with joy as Martin handed her a well-read Little Golden Book titled *Good Night, Little Bear.*

"One of my favorites," she whispered. Envy shifted to longing.

Lavinia was just finished cleaning up after dinner when Evelyn came down from reading. The two women went out to the screened porch to enjoy the evening and a pitcher of lemonade.

"What's wrong?" Lavinia asked.

Evelyn wasn't surprised that Lavinia could see how weary she was. "It's been a difficult year at school. How are your boys doing with the mandated integration and school closures?"

"Mandated what? I don't have the time for such nonsense. Our school board and the community have been fighting over this since 1956. You remember *Davis v. East Baton Rouge Parish School Board*? Now they're fooling with Freedom of Choice plans. Everyone's 'choosing' to be with their own. We put the boys in a segregated church school so we don't need to fuss. Anyway, I believe black teachers do a better job with black students."

Evelyn shook her head, thinking about Colleen. She was beginning to like the white woman but knew she needed to keep her distance. "But your family and then you were among the first to march against that school board decision. I don't understand. It's not like you to give up," Evelyn argued.

Lavinia had been actively involved in efforts to desegregate the schools with her parents. She had been one of the students who had participated in the early marches organized to demand equal access, materials, and supplies. The only marching Evelyn had done in college had been in the procession for their 1959 graduation.

"I didn't give up. I just looked for another way to get what I deserve and what our boys need. I'm still working as the library liaison for the elementary schools from the main branch of the Baton Rouge Library."

Evelyn felt her frustration mount. "You live in a big city. We're small-town country folks. That isn't an option for black families back in Kettle Creek or for me, either. We have to rely on the public schools. In one day, the school board destroyed what I had built for my students. Our school is locked up tight, and whatever I didn't grab that first day is gathering dust in my classroom. Now I teach in a white neighborhood, in a white environment. Nothing is comfortable. Everything has changed."

Lavinia took her friend's hand and said, "What do you want? It's time to live the life you want. You've given up so much for your family."

Evelyn thought about how she had returned to Kettle Creek after graduation to help her father and hadn't had any time for herself. "Good question: What *do* I want? I always thought only black teachers were best for our youngins, but the tide is turning."

"What's going on back there in Kettle Creek?" Lavinia asked.

"Integration is more complex than I ever could have imagined. I was mentoring this young white teacher before our school closed. At first I thought she was a foolish do-gooder, but she took her students, four at a time, to get library cards on Saturdays. She wants to know how to teach them, and she has some good ideas."

"Now, don't you go letting her think that she can do as good as you. Next thing you know, she'll be your boss. You know how that works."

◆◆◆

The ride back from Baton Rouge felt endless. The monotony of the road matched her thoughts as she ran through the conversations of the weekend. *What do I want?* She and Lavinia had both changed since college, and their long-awaited visit hadn't done the trick. Instead of lifting Evelyn's spirits, it had filled her with anger. That surprised her. Their first night together had confirmed their similarities and revealed their differences. Both women believed that black teachers were best for black students. She felt as if Lavinia was hiding from the legal battle her parents had started for Lavinia and her siblings' education. Evelyn had gone seeking answers from her friend and found that she already had them. She was the only black teacher who had kept her class in the crossover to the white school. She was proud of that and couldn't let her students down.

Lavinia's words kept running through her mind, even disrupting her sleep. Yes, Evelyn had gone home after graduation to help her father run the funeral home when her mother passed. True, she hadn't chosen that, but life had taken her on that path and she had accepted it. It had never felt like a burden. Teaching all week and serving families in mourning most weekends brought meaning to her life in ways she couldn't measure. She felt her anger rise again, remembering her friend say, "It's time to live the life you want." She *was*. Evelyn didn't want to marry. Lavinia had implied that her life was fuller with her husband and her sons. Evelyn loved children, but she was satisfied teaching and guiding them. She didn't need to have her own. For a brief moment, after reading *Good Night, Little Bear*, she had had a feeling of regret, as if something was missing. Something was. It was her students, the class she taught.

She realized how much she needed them *because* they needed her, especially this year. If she counted all her classes, she had taught hundreds of children. And many considered her a beloved auntie. Frank! She wondered how he had done with Mr. Fields. It was time to get back "to the life she had."

Chapter 32

●

Frank

Saturday, March 21, 1970

rank stopped polishing the chrome side bar to rise and
greet his new employer, Mr. Owen Fields.

"You sure like working on my new limousine, Frank."

"Yes, sir. I don't believe I've ever seen such a fine machine."

Frank knew that Mr. Fields was pleased with his latest purchase for the Glover Funeral Home. Maintaining it so it shone
could help Frank keep his job. The used 1960 Cadillac Landau
hearse had leather upholstery and an automatic transmission.
Frank used any excuse to get under the hood to admire the
325-horsepower, V8 engine. It helped him to come to terms with
his resistance to car repair. Everything his father had taught
him was paying off. He was a natural.

"Do you like to drive, Frank?"

Frank folded the chamois. "Yes, I do."

"Have you ever driven anything besides your mother's old
car?"

Frank remembered how he used to drive with his father in

the old pickup and the times he had helped to haul hay with the tractor on Ole Man Everett's farm.

"Does a tractor count?"

"I'm sure it does," Mr. Fields replied. The corners of his eyes crinkled as he held back laughter. "I could use another driver on Saturdays, now that I have this hearse. Would you like to try to drive it?"

Frank's father had taught him to drive when he was only fourteen. But this was a professional car.

"Frank? What do you think?"

He couldn't believe it. He thought he had responded. But Mr. Fields was still waiting.

"Yes!"

"Good. You'll need a suit if you're driving for us. Do you have one?"

"No, sir, I don't." Awed at the idea of imitating the professionally dressed black man who was now his boss, Frank wondered if his father had ever owned a suit. He couldn't recall ever having seen him in one.

"This might take us a bit of time. I would like you to take me for a drive each day you work until you can handle the hearse comfortably. In the meantime, we'll work on finding a suit for you. The bereaved families often offer the driver additional compensation. How does that sound?"

Mr. Fields extended his hand, and Frank took it in a firm grasp.

"I won't let you down, Mr. Fields. Thank you for the offer."

"Good day to you, son." Mr. Fields nodded as he walked away.

Frank turned back and continued polishing the car with feverish energy, thinking about how the extra money would help him build up his new savings account. Just the prior month, he had almost fallen for the army recruiter's spiel at the school assembly. The man had claimed that the benefits for enlisting included college tuition.

Chapter 33

♠

Colleen

Monday, March 30, 1970

"Ten weeks—that's all we have left. June sixth, we're gone."
Ten weeks?

The week off from school had given her time to plan. Miguel had ten weeks left until active-duty discharge. He had served his time and was ready to return to New Jersey and his career. But she had only nine weeks left with her students and was excited to get back to school, where they would continue their work on cursive writing. The first letters they learned were *c*, *o*, *a*, *d*, and *g*. They were motivated when they joined letters to write a few words, like *dog* and *add*.

Even though the Dick and Jane books were old and out-of-date, the workbooks had assessments at the end, as did the math workbooks. The assessments documented improvement in reading and math skills. Each child had a black-and-white marble composition pad filled with writing samples. All she had to do was turn the pages to see the changes. Over spring break, she had reviewed their work and felt good about their progress.

May 29 was the last day of school. She wanted to make these the best nine weeks of the school year.

She loaded a cardboard box with the materials she had collected for planting bean seeds. She needed to make two trips to the car to bring in the books about plants. Jeanne, her new librarian friend, had collected more than she had space for, but Colleen took them anyway.

As she was clearing her desktop, the only spot large enough to set up the materials for the bean planting, Cynthia burst into the trailer.

"Miz Rodriguez, I'm glad to see you." Her little frame was heaving with breathlessness. Colleen didn't have a chance to ask why before Linkston came up the wooden steps and through the open door.

"You cain't leave the door open. All the cold air will escape!" he shouted.

Colleen held in a laugh. It was good to see these two. Nothing had changed with them. Now she knew the reason for the heavy breathing. Cynthia and Linkston had raced from the street. Cynthia had won again.

"Did you two come on the bus today? It's early for you to be here already."

"No, my mama has a new job, and she brought us in the car," Cynthia announced.

"I'm glad to see you. I can use some help. Do you want to set up the library table or the science experiment?"

"Science experiment!" they both shouted.

"First, let's put these newspapers on the top of my desk. Okay?"

Colleen handed them each a section of newspaper and demonstrated how to take two or three sheets and layer them to cover the desk.

"Happy Easter, Miz Rodriguez. Do you like my new dress?" Cynthia asked, as she tidily set down the papers. "I wore it to church yesterday, and my mama said I could wear it today to show you. I had a hat, too, but I couldn't wear that to school—it might get ruined."

The skirt of her dress ballooned as she spun around.

"I love it, Cynthia, especially the bow in the back. It's fancy—"

"I'm done. Used all the newspapers," Linkston interrupted, clearly annoyed with all the chatter about Cynthia's dress.

"That's great. Now you can take out the paper cups. Please lift them up out of the box carefully so the dirt doesn't spill out of them."

On the desktop, Colleen placed the container of lima beans that she had soaked overnight, along with paper towels, sandwich bags, a black marker, and a spray bottle full of water. She checked her watch. "I'm glad you came early. The science project is all set up. Let's go get the class."

An unfamiliar emotion filled Colleen as they made their way out of the trailer: a sudden burst of joy at the challenge of the unplanned integration, the rejection by the staff at the white school, the lack of materials, and the impossibly tight quarters, in comparison with what she had accomplished despite all that. Cynthia and Linkston were two good examples. Pride nudged the happiness in her heart when she saw the lineup of smiling faces waiting for her.

The safety of the prepared science project was compromised as soon as Jarrod saw Colleen's desktop. He picked up the spray bottle of water. "Miz Rodriguez, what's all this stuff for?"

"Please put it down. It's for our science lesson after lunch." She wasn't sure who was more amazed when he did exactly what she asked.

Everyone seemed glad to be back to the school routine, and the morning went smoothly. As promised, the science experiment was the first of the afternoon activities. Colleen stood behind her desk and explained that they were going to plant some bean seeds in soil and some in a plastic bag without soil.

"Y'all need to put them beans in dirt," Jarrod called out.

Of course, Colleen thought. *Did he use up all his goodness in the morning?*

"That is the usual way, Jarrod, but this is an experiment, and we're going to find out what plants need to grow. We're going to observe and compare. Those are science words. Are you ready to be scientists?"

"Yes!" they yelled in a gleeful chorus. Colleen guided the children to place three beans in the cup and cover them gently with soil. They each folded a paper towel, and then Colleen sprayed it with water. She demonstrated how to put the towel in the plastic sandwich bag, lay three more beans on the towel, and fold over the top of the bag. She taped the bags to the wall behind her desk. "We're going to take the beans we planted in the cups outside and put them next to the steps in this box. The outside beans in dirt will have light and water each day. The inside beans in the bags will have water. It's your job to watch them grow."

The first two days of the week after spring break felt like her days back at West Hill School. The fine-tuning of her classroom management had them all humming, literally. Colleen was her old self. She burst into song to signal the class. If she sang "A Beautiful Morning," they knew to pick up their carpets "to go outside awhile"; when she sang "Yellow Submarine," it was because they needed a break. She and the class would march single file through the rows of desks. Pretending the trailer was a submarine beneath the sea fed everyone's resilience.

Chapter 34

*

Colleen

Wednesday, April 1, 1970

It was April Fools' Day. Colleen wondered who would try to play a joke. Each afternoon's routine now included checking the beans. On the way back from lunch, Colleen instructed the children to pick up their beans in the cups and observe. They observed whether the soil was damp and whether they could spot any growth. The children were disappointed that nothing had happened.

"It takes a while for the roots to pop out. You can't see them under the dirt. Let's check the ones in the bags inside."

Colleen was glad that the fluorescent lights in the classroom provided enough light that some of the beans in the bags had started to sprout in just three days. No one had noticed in the morning.

"There isn't enough room for all of us to observe the bags taped to the bulletin board. Row one, would you please be our first observers?"

Seven children crowded around the bulletin board in the back of their classroom.

"Miz Rodriguez, I see some squiggly white roots popping out of my bean," Jarrod said.

"Excellent observation. Did your bean in the cup have any roots, Jarrod?"

He shook his head.

"What do you think is happening in the cup?"

He shrugged his shoulders.

"Take a guess, Jarrod."

"Maybe my bean has roots?"

"That's right. We couldn't see the roots in the cup because they're under the dirt, but we should see the green shoots pop out soon."

His smile was so broad that it filled his face and Colleen's heart. He had finally gained confidence. "I'm proud of you, Jarrod. You took a chance, and you were right."

By the end of the day, Colleen was surprised that not one child had played an April Fools' joke. Did they know about it? She would find out.

"Children, before we go home, I have a surprise for you, but I need you all to be seated and looking at me. Are you ready?"

She reviewed the bean-planting process and reminded them that even if you don't have dirt, seeds can sprout. She handed out filled sandwich bags to each child.

"Take a look. What do you see in the bags?"

"It looks like cereal," Linkston said.

"Cheerios," Cynthia added.

"Oh, no, that's not what these are," Colleen said. "They're seeds."

"Miz Rodriguez, these are not seeds. These here are for breakfast," Jarrod said.

"No, these are special seeds—these are donut seeds. Didn't you ever hear about donut seeds? If you take good care of them like you did with the bean seeds, you can have a crop of donuts."

Thirty pairs of hungry eyes popped as wide as their open mouths.

"What flavors? Chocolate?" Jarrod asked.

Excited children looked at each other and shook their filled bags.

"Strawberry frosted?" a hesitant voice called out from the back.

Cynthia held up her bag of Cheerios and said, "Y'all, these seeds are vanilla."

Linkston shook his head in disbelief and caught Colleen's eye.

She winked at him and said, "April Fools'!"

They laughed. "You tricked us!"

Unfazed, Jarrod asked, "Miz Rodriguez, can we eat them?"

"Yes. Enjoy the donut seeds, everyone."

Chapter 35

🍎

Colleen

Friday, May 15, 1970

C olleen was at the back of the trailer when Jarrod called out, "Miz Rodriguez, Miz Rodriguez, someone is knocking."

The lack of windows made it impossible to see anything but the four walls of the trailer classroom. No one knocked for long, if at all. Typically, any visitor just came in and interrupted whatever they were in the middle of. Colleen opened the door outward to see a tall white boy standing below the first step. He knew to stand low so that the door wouldn't hit him when it opened. As Colleen stepped back to let him enter the class-room, he reached up and handed her a note. He left without speaking.

The children were as curious as Colleen.

Jarrod called out again, "What does it say, Miz Rodriguez?"

Linkston looked at her with worried eyes behind his glasses. "Are you in trouble, Miz Rodriguez?"

Shifting her stance, Colleen opened the paper. "Now, why would you think that, Linkston?" But as she read the note, she wondered the same thing.

It was a request to meet the principal in his office after the children were dismissed for the day.

That afternoon, the office was bustling. A few of the PTA parents were placing pale blue envelopes, each topped with a tiny fresh-flower nosegay, inside the teachers' mail cubbies. At the same time, some of the teachers were checking for any notices before they left for the weekend. Chatter about Friday night plans made the office a lively and deceivingly pleasant place.

Colleen watched one teacher open the envelope as she gushed, "How lovely of you ladies, treating all the teachers so kindly with a luncheon at the end of the school year. Thank you for the invitation and for the flowers."

Several other teachers reached to retrieve theirs, crowding the passage through the office. Colleen had to excuse herself several times to move out of the path of the mutual admiration society of chattering teachers and parents.

When she finally reached the secretary's desk, she was greeted with a curt directive. "He's waiting for you, Mrs. Rodriguez. Go right in."

The door to the office had a textured glass window designed to filter light and provide privacy. His name was etched into the glass.

The afternoon sun blinded her as she sat in the chair he pointed to. He barely lifted his head as he continued to examine a stack of papers on the desktop. She could see his scalp through his thinning hair. He seemed annoyed; Colleen wondered what she had done to receive such a reception.

Mr. Palmer finally looked up at her over wire-framed eyeglasses perched on the tip of his nose and said, "Mrs. Rodriguez, we have decided that all the C-level classes will not be passed on. Your students are not prepared for third grade. They are to be retained, and you need to inform the parents. I've prepared a letter for you to copy and sign."

Colleen froze. "Excuse me, sir. I don't understand."

"You don't need to understand. We cannot pass these poor Negro children to third grade unprepared and allow them to continue a life of failure."

"Failure?" She leaned forward. "Then you don't know my students, Mr. Palmer. They have all moved up at least two reading levels since I started teaching in August. They know all the Dolch sight words." She pushed back her chair. "I should have brought my charts and their writing samples with me. The improvement is quite clear. I'll get them for you."

His response chilled her. "No, that will not be necessary."

"But . . ."

He stopped her with a stern look as he removed his glasses.

"I'm only trying to explain . . ."

He didn't let her speak about math, science, or social studies. "Mrs. Rodriguez, you are bordering on insubordination."

"Sir . . ."

"Aren't you planning to return to New Jersey after the school year? I expect that you will want a letter of recommendation from me. They will be retained. This is out of your hands. Have the letters ready to send home on Monday."

He dismissed her with a wave of his hand and picked up the phone. She stood up slowly, willing her tears not to flow as she went to open the office door.

Colleen composed herself, pretended nothing was wrong, and went over to sign out and get her mail. The gaggle of women who had been standing around the mailboxes had departed. As she sorted through flyers and end-of-year paperwork, she realized that she hadn't received a pale blue envelope containing an invitation to the teacher luncheon, nor a tiny fresh-flower nosegay.

Chapter 36

♦

Annie Mae

Saturday, May 16, 1970

Annie Mae was looking forward to the end of this school year. It had been difficult, but prayers had pulled her through. Her husband, Shelton, must be bursting with pride from his grave. Frank was finding his way to college without the football scholarship they had counted on. Frank had stayed out of the protest walkouts his friends had organized. She knew it was because of her; he didn't want her ever to have to pick him up at the jail again. The job he had gotten at the funeral home wouldn't be enough to pay for college, but she saw how determined he was. He'd manage somehow.

Walking through her living room with her dustcloth, she picked up her wedding picture. Frank was a lot like his father. Shelton was one of a few army veterans from the Korean War who believed his town was ready for change. Fred Peterson was another. Annie Mae put the picture back when her eyes filled with tears. She didn't have time to be sad.

Saturday mornings were hers. Today she was the only one home. Up since dawn, she had just finished cleaning the kitchen. Her daughters didn't understand why she polished the top of the refrigerator every week, but that was how she liked it—no dust balls would ever float down into her cooking.

Annie Mae took care of several white families' cleaning and ironing all week, and she had her own four children to look after too. The day was hot, and she promised herself a tall glass of iced tea on the porch when she was finished with her chores.

Frank had left the house early to drive the hearse for a funeral. Sissy had taken Rachel and Baby James over to the horse farm to see the newest colt. Shelton's cousin Penelope had invited them to come early and stay for lunch.

Penelope had inherited the family farm and the horses from her grandmother and namesake. She visited regularly but lived and worked in Manhattan, where she sold real estate properties to professional Negro families. She had found her way out of their small town years ago but never forgot where she came from. Penelope employed a caretaker and his family to manage the farm.

Annie Mae heard the mail truck and the familiar slams of seven roadside mailboxes as the postman rushed through the delivery. She decided to take a break. On the way down the shady driveway to collect her mail, she plucked a few weeds from her flower bed. When she pulled open the hinged door to the box, a crisp white business-size envelope rested on the top of the pile. She took it out to read the return address of the parish school board and saw the formal, typed recipient's name: Mrs. Annie M. Woods.

Chapter 37

●

Frank

Saturday, May 16, 1970

F rank hurried home from work. He didn't want to miss Dedra's call about some graduation plans the Black Student Committee had put together. His friendship with Dedra had been renewed ever since she had seen him in his suit. He had driven the hearse at her aunt's funeral two weeks earlier. Frank generally tried to stay in the background, but that day Mr. Fields had had him assist the family into their cars. Dedra hadn't seen him at first. They hadn't spoken since he had refused to be part of the walkout. But her face had softened when their eyes met, and she'd said, "So, this is where you've been keeping yourself, Frank. Quite a change from that football uniform, I'd say."

Now he hurried out as soon as Mr. Fields closed the door on the last mourner. Frank drove home from the funeral home without trading his suit pants for the jeans he usually wore. The driver's seat of his mother's car was worn, but he had examined it for any snags before sitting down. He folded the jacket and laid it carefully on the passenger seat. He couldn't afford another suit. The job took up all of his after-school and weekend time, but he had been able to save some money.

As he drove his mother's old '53 Crown Victoria up the road to his house, Frank noticed the row of mailboxes. Theirs was left open. He looked and saw nothing inside, so he snapped the small door shut.

"Ma! I'm home! I'm starving. What's for dinner?"

He found her sitting in her wing chair, as she called it, the one with the brown-striped velvet upholstery. She was holding a piece of paper, and a long white envelope was on her lap.

"I need you to read this, and then we can talk. Please sit with me."

"Ma, can't I change my clothes and then read it?"

"No. Sit with me, Frank."

He looked at his mother's dull eyes, the tight set of her jaw, and realized that the paper in her hand didn't bear good news. As he sat down, she handed him the letter:

Dear Mrs. Woods,

The parish school board has made the decision to require all seniors from West Hill High School to attend a fifth year at Kettle Creek High School. This generous offer will assure that all students receive a full curriculum before graduation. This decision will delay the graduation date for your son, Franklin Delano Woods, until the completion of the 1970–71 school year.

Sincerely,

Mr. Cornelius Palmer

Principal, Kettle Creek High School

Frank shifted his body in the chair and read it again. It didn't make sense. He leaped up, unable to contain the anger boiling inside him.

"They can't do this to me, Ma!" *Peterson and his promises.* "Damn honkies do what they want. First, they cut me from the team? And now no graduation?"

One look from her, and he settled down. What she said next shocked him.

"Frank, I've been sitting here and praying on this. We *cannot* let this happen. I don't know how to stop it, but we'll find a way."

Chapter 38

♠

Colleen

Saturday, May 16, 1970

"Hi, Dad. I can't believe it. I have to send a letter to the parents of each student in my class to let them know I'm retaining their child. The principal wrote the letter, but I have to make copies and sign it. It's awful! 'Dear Parents, this is to inform you that your child will not be passed to third grade, so that the school can provide them with additional time to meet the challenging curriculum of Kettle Creek Elementary.' Ridiculous."

She pressed the STOP button. Staring at the recorder, Colleen gave up on the idea of talking it out with her father. He would never get the tape in time to give her advice. She was just talking to herself. What was the point?

Big, fat, quiet tears rolled down her cheeks and dripped onto the tape player.

Where are those cigarettes? Damn! Of all the weekends for Miguel to be away on maneuvers! Who can I talk to? Evelyn?

Evelyn had the same problem she did because she had the below-level 3C class. No phone meant having to drive to the pay phone or using the one in their landlord's house. And she didn't want anyone to overhear what she was saying. She found the carton of Marlboros. *The last pack.* Colleen chain-smoked until the surge of nicotine soothed her anxiety.

She considered her options: write the letters or don't write the letters. If she sent the letters, she was ignoring the success and progress of the year. If she didn't send them, would it matter? She had no authority to pass her students on to third grade. Worse, she had no power. Send the letter. It was the only way to expose how unfair the decision was. She'd have to rely on her students' parents to do something.

Colleen didn't have a typewriter in the trailer. She would have to type the letter at school. Thinking about asking the secretary if she could use her typewriter changed her mind. Colleen didn't want to sit at that woman's desk. It would be like sitting in a fishbowl. She imagined the unfriendly secretary watching her and knew that she would only make mistake after mistake, wasting the dittos, pulling the ditto master out of the typewriter, and getting purple ink all over her hands. Colleen decided she would just have to write it carefully by hand onto the master. The more she thought through the steps, the clearer her plan got. It would have to be in cursive and sealed in an envelope. The children would be able to read it if she typed it.

Yes! Many of them will be able to read it! Yet the principal didn't even want to know about them.

After lunch on Monday, Colleen made copies of her handwritten letter, stuffed the envelopes, and addressed each one. At the end of the day, she inserted each letter into the folders she used to send homework and school notices home.

"Miz Rodriguez, why are we bringing letters home? Is that my report card?"

Of course Jarrod would be worried about a letter going home.

"No, Jarrod, it's a special notice for your parents. Report cards go home next week."

"I was worried, Miz Rodriguez. You always show us our report cards first. My mama doesn't like bad news. I want to see it before she does."

"You will, Jarrod, next week."

As Colleen lined up the students and took them out to the bus lines, she wondered how his mother and all the parents would react.

The report cards are worthless, and so am I.

Chapter 39

●

Annie Mae

Monday, May 18, 1970

"Hello, Mr. Peterson. I'm calling to ask if you're free to join Reverend Wilford and some parents at the church this evening," Annie Mae Woods said. A baseball game played loudly in the background. The volume was so high, she could hear the announcer: "Astros lead one to zero, top of the second." She was relieved to hear him agree.

Annie Mae had asked the reverend if he could meet with her and some of the parents. Folks were getting the news about the canceled high school graduation by word of mouth, and the location and purpose of the meeting kept changing as the day went on and more people wanted to attend.

First, all the seniors—fifty-three of them—had been told that they couldn't graduate. Their parents were ready to storm the parish school board offices. That was bad enough. But when the elementary-school children had come home from school on Monday with letters explaining that they would all be retained, the group had gotten larger and angrier.

Annie Mae arrived early to prop open the heavy, solid oak

doors as an invitation to enter Tabernacle Baptist Church. She made herself stop to admire the carved panels depicting the life of Jesus, her hands passing over the impressive craftsmanship with gentle, loving strokes. Shelton had teased the figures from the wood long ago, but his essence remained. His artistic skills and time had served as their tithing to the church.

The reverend would lead the meeting once everyone arrived. Mr. Peterson's presence would help calm tempers. Annie Mae prayed that folks would have more self-control in the church than they'd had on the phone.

"Good evening, Reverend," Annie Mae called when he entered from the rear door. He paced up and down the aisle, scanning the pews for stray missals, replacing them in the bookracks. He was tense and distracted.

The reverend offered quiet greetings at the door as the community streamed into the church. Soon the pews were filled. Annie Mae sat up front, turning each time someone entered. Hope filled her heart when she saw the figure she had been waiting for. The woman's ebony skin glistened in the heat of the evening. A wide, colorful band above her forehead held her full, high Afro in place. Large gold hoop earrings swung as she walked to take a seat next to Annie Mae.

Chapter 40

🍎

Colleen

Tuesday, May 19, 1970

When Colleen met the children at their bus line on Tuesday morning it was clear how badly the letters had been received. They stared silently at her, waiting for her to say the first word. The usual banter and chatter were absent. Her customary "Good morning, chickadees!" blew away with the wind.

The children followed her into the classroom trailer like ducks in a line. All were surprisingly compliant and meek, except, of course, for Jarrod, who finally spoke up: "Miz Rodriguez, my mama says I can't go to third grade. You told me I was doing good."

As Colleen struggled to reply, Rachel handed her an envelope. "My mama told me to give you this letter. I'm supposed to listen to you and do my work."

Colleen read the letter from Annie Mae Woods. It requested that Colleen meet with Annie Mae's cousin Penelope Woods after school.

The hum of the air conditioner was the loudest noise in the trailer. The day dragged along as the children and Colleen struggled with their work. Rachel was true to her mama's advice, but she didn't volunteer a sound all day long, not even raising her hand when Colleen asked for sentences for the spelling words. Rachel loved to write and read the longest sentence by using more than one of the words from the list. The tracks of tears on Cynthia's cheeks replaced her usual gleeful shouts when she got the correct answer. And when Colleen put a sticker on Linkston's perfect math paper, his smile started and then stopped as their eyes met.

The day was finally over. Sad, disappointed faces broke her heart as she dismissed her students. After they boarded their buses, Colleen walked back to her classroom to meet with Annie Mae's cousin. It was only a few minutes before she heard a rapping knock. A surge of adrenaline replaced Colleen's anxiety as she opened the door. A tall black woman with a huge Afro hairstyle stood on the path to the steps. Dressed professionally in a pantsuit, with a large gold sunburst necklace and big hoop earrings, she looked like cover girl Naomi Sims with a bit of Angela Davis mixed in. Fear gripped Colleen as she recalled newsreels and newspaper and magazine photographs. Her mind shifted to black power marches that started as nonviolent demonstrations. Visions of dogs attacking Negroes and grown white men hosing the marchers up against a wall competed with her trust that Mrs. Woods wouldn't send anyone who would harm her. But she didn't know why this woman was here and couldn't help wondering, *Who is this? What's her story?*

The woman extended her hand and introduced herself. "Good afternoon. I'm Penelope Woods. May we speak?"

Colleen gulped as she opened the door wider to allow the woman to come up the steps. "Yes . . . Yes, of course."

"I was at a meeting last night and met one of your principals,

Mr. Peterson. I told him that I was coming to speak to you today. He was glad to hear it."

That news surprised Colleen but didn't stop the pounding in her chest. She nervously pulled out her desk chair for Penelope. It was the only adult-size chair in the room. Colleen sat on a student desk and apologized for the lack of space.

"Miz Rodriguez, your apologies aren't necessary. I am here to represent the children of my cousins, Rachel Woods and Linkston Jefferson. Annie Mae has also asked me to speak for the other parents. Please tell me, why are you retaining your entire class?"

She didn't waste any time. The anxiety returned and rushed through Colleen, making it hard for her to remain seated as she stumbled into an answer.

Colleen explained the directive she had been given, making no effort to protect Cornelius Palmer. She rose to gather all the things she'd wanted to bring to the principal: her grade book, the charts of sight words, and the science and social studies projects on the bulletin boards. At least someone would get to see her proof of progress.

Penelope listened and then asked, "Where are you from?"

Colleen told her, and Penelope nodded. "Yes, New Jersey. I thought I recognized your accent."

Penelope stood and began to walk around the room. Colleen realized how tall she was when the woman's hair brushed the ceiling.

"I live and work in New York City, but I own a horse farm here, which is why I'm in town."

She fingered the papers tacked to the bulletin board and studied the bar graphs that tallied the number of books each student had read. She seemed preoccupied as she gazed at the display.

"So, Miz Rodriguez, I will explain to the parents what you have told me. While they are not happy, this is a bigger problem than your second-grade class. Another teacher who lives in our community, Evelyn Glover, had the same meeting with the principal. Her story is the same as yours. But she handled it differently. In addition, over the weekend, my cousin Annie Mae Woods received a letter. Her son Frank and all the black high school seniors are not going to be allowed to graduate."

"I didn't know. How could they do that?" Colleen realized how broad this decision had been, when she had been thinking only about herself and her class. What had Evelyn done differently? Was there another option? If the decision to retain students included high school seniors, what was next?

Colleen shifted off the desktop and stood on shaky legs to extend her hand first, in hopes of ending the meeting.

"Thank you for speaking with me. Please tell the parents that I'm sincerely sorry. This has been upsetting to me, and I know it's been upsetting to the children."

"I see that, Miz Rodriguez. I realize that you're nothing more than a pawn in this game. But we're not finished."

Chapter 41

●

Frank

Tuesday, May 19, 1970

The phone rang. These days, it was always ringing. His mother answered and, after a second, called him.

"Frank, it's for you. Don't be long. I'm expecting a call."

If she had seen him roll his eyes, she wouldn't have given him the phone. He picked it up from the counter and opened the pantry door as she walked outside to gather the clothes drying on the line.

When he heard Dedra's voice on the other end, he smiled and said, "I've been waiting for you to call since Saturday."

"That's exactly what I've been doing, Frank. But either there was no answer or it was busy. Why didn't you call me?"

"Can't get near the phone. My mother has been talking to every parent, teacher, neighbor, preacher she can. She's not telling me what they're doing, but I know they're going to the parish school board meeting Thursday night."

"That's why I'm calling. Forget about the Black Student Committee and our meetings with Mr. Palmer. He sent that letter to all of us two days after he claimed he'd consider our request to graduate from our own high school. We're going to the school with food and blankets on Thursday night."

His mother came back into the house. The sounds from the kitchen were quiet and soft; she must be folding the laundry on the table.

"Are you there?" Dedra asked.

He remembered the pain of the foot on his back when the police had stopped the students' protest walk. He felt the twist of the handcuffs on his wrists.

"Yes, I hear you."

He relived the anguish of sitting in the jail cell waiting for his mother.

"Well? Are you in this time? We're meeting at dusk behind the building, and we're not leaving until they let us graduate."

His mind raced. Heat rose to his forehead as he recalled the shame of being placed on second string because of his skin color, and now being told he couldn't graduate.

His temples throbbed; his heart pounded. Taking a deep breath, he squared his shoulders. "Yes, I'll be there. I've got to go now. See you Thursday."

He slowly opened the door from the pantry, relieved to see the kitchen empty. Folded laundry lay in neat piles on the table. He gently placed the phone on the hook and walked out.

In his bedroom, he pulled the second drawer out of his bureau, placed it on the bed, and reached into the empty space. His heartbeat steadied as his fingers grasped the small metal rectangle resting on the drawer's support rail. The lighter was the same width as the rail, and the drawer could still close each time he took it out.

His bedroom was exactly the same now as it had been before the fire. He studied the single wall covered with the striped wallpaper his father had helped him paste up. They had never finished the job.

Memories of the fire flooded his mind. His thumb rubbed the grooved surface of the inexpensive Zippo lighter. He always woke up in a sweat from the dream. Awake, he couldn't erase his father's body being placed in the pickup, his shoe left behind on the ground, or the silver glint next to the shoe. His recurring dream was a reality and a memory he couldn't reconcile.

As he clutched the lighter, he felt his father's presence, as well as his own anger, his guilt, and his fear. He'd never told anyone he had found it. Each time he took it from its hiding spot, he asked his father what to do. The lighter had become his confessional. If he had given the lighter to the FBI, would anything have changed?

The town police never came to investigate his father's death. But FBI agents knocked on his mother's door a few months later, after the NAACP filed a complaint. He was fourteen and scared, watching from the hallway. He heard his mother gasp when she saw Reverend Wilford with two white men dressed in jackets and ties, with fedoras on their heads.

"It's all right, Mrs. Woods. I asked them to come. We're sorry to bother you. They just have a few questions." Frank remembered seeing the short and portly reverend move forward to stand in front of the agents.

"May I offer you some tea and cake?" Frank heard the tightness in his mother's voice. It was the first and last time she invited any white men to sit down for tea with her.

"Miz Woods, that won't be necessary. We can sit in the parlor without any refreshments," the reverend said.

At the same time, the man who Frank would learn was the

lead agent said, "Thank you, ma'am. I hate to bother you, but I would appreciate some tea and your kind hospitality."

As he thought back now, Frank realized that the agent's gesture of kindness, perhaps a false extension of sympathy, had given them more time in the house.

The teacups clinked against the saucers while Frank's mother served from the tray she was carrying. He had seen her serve tea many times with a steady hand and comfortable conversation. This time, fear rattled the cups.

As they sat in the parlor, the lead agent's big hands were surprisingly agile as he placed the delicate cup down and nodded to his partner to take off his hat.

"We're trying to determine the cause of the fire. Is there anything you can tell us? Was your husband having trouble with anyone?" The agent spoke in a low voice, perhaps trying to soften his questions or his presence.

Annie Mae just shook her head. She had answers, but she wouldn't share what she knew. She was too frightened. Just having the FBI in the house put the family's safety at risk.

"We know he was a vet and had some friends on both sides of the Mississippi. Have they been here to see you?" The lead agent took another sip of tea as he waited for her answer.

Frank wondered where this man was from. Didn't he know that the white mechanics his father worked with wouldn't come to the house? Ever? Even though he was a top-notch mechanic whom they sought out and hired? Maybe he had served, but that didn't matter. He had been a civilian when he died—someone who lived on the wrong side of town, not on the army base.

"No, sir, just our friends from church and our neighbors." Annie Mae lifted a plate of sliced cake to offer the agents. "Our community has been a great comfort. My friend Evelyn made this cake."

The other agent balanced his hat on his knee as he reached for a slice of cake and finally spoke. "Have any of the NAACP members come to visit?"

Annie Mae looked toward the reverend for some support.

"Miz Woods just told you that only neighbors and friends from our church have been to visit. I think it's time for us to take our leave now."

The lead agent nodded but asked, "Is there anything else you can tell us, Mrs. Woods?"

She shook her head and looked away.

He took the reverend's advice and stood. "Thank you for your time, Mrs. Woods. Here's my card. Please call me if you change your mind."

The memory of his mother shaking her head made Frank recall the reason she had been so quiet. His father's army buddy, another Korean War vet, had died in a truck explosion over in Natchez. His father had been the third Korean War vet with connections to the Natchez branch of the NAACP and Armstrong Rubber Company to die. Frank knew that the fire wasn't an accident. The men involved in killing him would find a way to hurt Frank, his sisters, or his mother if they helped the FBI. He was sure of that.

All this time, he had hidden the lighter. Would anyone believe it had anything to do with the fire if he handed it over to the FBI four years later?

The lighter's surface was scratched and well used, but three engraved letters were visible: BNH. Frank knew it was time to do something, even if he was afraid. Instead of putting the lighter back in the hiding place, he slid it into his pocket and went to find his mother, to tell her that he was going with Dedra on Thursday.

Chapter 42

♥

Colleen

Tuesday, May 19, 1970

C olleen parked the car next to the trailer and was grateful when she heard the hum of the air conditioner. Miguel was home.

"You're an hour late. I was getting worried about you."

"Yeah, me too. The day was awful. It ended okay, but I seriously thought I was in mortal danger."

Alarmed, he stopped what he was doing and came over to her. He put his arm around her, and they sat down on the couch. She was grateful for the closeness of his body and the cool air that flowed over them.

"Things got worse," she told him.

"What happened?"

Colleen told him how upset the children were, about Rachel's note, and how every time she looked at Cynthia, she had to hold back her own tears.

"They hate me. I've totally let them down. They will never believe a white woman again in their lives. You should have seen how they looked at me."

"School will be over in two weeks, and we're going home in eighteen days."

Home. A place where she understood the rules, even if she didn't always agree with them.

She told him about her meeting with Penelope. Miguel was a good listener but wasn't one to give a lot of advice. He kept things to himself. She never had.

Colleen thought about her husband's way of dealing with unfair situations. He just pushed forward, didn't dwell on what he couldn't change. He couldn't change Castro's broken promises and Cuba's shift to communism. He couldn't change his parents' decision to flee from their beloved country or his draft status after college. He had no choice but to accept his two years in the army. Now he was ready to go home to New Jersey and start the life they had planned.

"Well, quit, then. I don't know how you did it this long."

"I can't run away from this. You wouldn't. I can handle it—I have to handle it."

"Colleen, I don't know what to say or how to help you."

"Just hold me."

All day long, she had wanted to cry. Now she could, but the tears wouldn't come.

Chapter 43

❤

Evelyn

Thursday, May 21, 1970

E velyn smoothed her shirtwaist dress as she got behind the wheel of her car. She took a deep breath to calm herself. How many board meetings had she attended as the liaison for the Parent Teacher Association? But this one was different. She had been powerless, but now she had a plan. She had been told to retain her class, just like Colleen and two other teachers. Except for the student walkouts, the desegregation of the Kettle Creek Schools had avoided more serious confrontations and personal injury. Tonight could be different. Even Annie Mae was riled up. She was the force behind the group that was insisting on an emergency meeting of the school board.

As Evelyn drove along the unpaved streets of her neighborhood, she passed small groups of students walking toward the main road. She noticed that they were carrying blankets. Puzzled, she stopped her car. As she rolled down the window to speak to a group, one of them came over to her. It was Sissy, Frank's sister, and right behind her were her friends Kendra and Pearl.

"Sissy, where are you going?"

"Oh, hi, Miz Glover. We're just walking to our high school to meet some friends."

"With blankets? Does your mama know what you're doing?"

"No, she left the house right after dinner for the parish school board meeting."

Kendra and Pearl stood back, whispering to each other, shifting from one foot to the other as they waited for Sissy. They looked nervous.

Evelyn called them over. "Where are your manners? Don't you greet your old third-grade teacher?"

As the girls approached the car, Evelyn could see that they also had food wrapped in bags under the blankets they were balancing. She realized the rumors must be true: the students were on the way to their old high school and were prepared to stay.

"Oh, Miz Glover, please don't tell us to go home. We have to go."

Evelyn was impressed that these children, as she still thought of them, had the courage to stand with the seniors to protest the graduation decision. She was on her way to the board meeting to do the same. Even if she told them to leave, she knew they'd just return after she drove away. They had more spirit than she did. The year had worn her down. And she worried about what the next year would bring.

Evelyn recalled a recent newspaper interview with the superintendent, which described the "professionalism" of teachers who had worked through the closing and the unifying of the Kettle Creek Schools. The superintendent credited the staff for the smooth transition. "We should hire good teachers, pay them well, and provide them with the tools they need. . . . The keys to good schools are good teachers. . . . Failure in schools is due to teachers who are not flexible, who don't have enthusiasm or love for the children."

Clearly, he didn't know the staff at West Hill Elementary. He had hired good teachers. If the school board had provided them with the tools they needed, things would have been better. Would any teachers retire or move away after this school year? Evelyn wondered what would happen to her.

"Miz Glover, are you okay?" Sissy's voice brought her back to the present. She realized the girls were staring at her silently.

"Promise me you'll be careful and run home if there's any trouble. Can you do that?"

"We promise, Miz Glover."

Evelyn left the girls and drove onto the pavement with a worried heart. She knew that Annie Mae would not be happy with her decision to let them go. Annie Mae thought her daughter was home, but at least Evelyn knew where Sissy really was. *Who's watching Rachel and Baby James? Oh, Lordy, did I do the right thing?*

As she passed the high school, she saw that it was still boarded up and locked. The only lights were from the streetlamps near the parking lot. Students were quietly gathering in the side yard, laying down blankets. It looked peaceful, as if they were going to have a picnic.

The five-mile drive down Highway 179 seemed longer than usual and very still. She scanned the road. Shouldn't there be more traffic? She tapped her fingers on the steering wheel. How many folks would be there? That question was answered as she searched for a parking spot. Was she late? Had she missed it? The lot was full; some cars were on the lawn, and a few were parked diagonally along the side roads, making it difficult to pass. She finally found a spot past the white high school and had to walk two blocks to Kettle Creek Elementary.

Chapter 44

🍎

Colleen

Thursday, May 21, 1970

No wonder school ended in May. The heat and humidity of the Louisiana days were ramping up. Tension and stress in the cramped classroom had doubled since the previous Friday. It was time to go home and work on packing before dinner. Colleen shut down the AC, locked the door, and walked to her car. She was amazed at how much she and Miguel had accumulated in one year. The army would ship the boxes home, but she had to fill them. "Ten weeks—that's all we have left. June sixth, we're gone," Miguel had said. June 6 was just two weeks away.

The second bedroom, at the back end of the trailer, was where she organized the packing. She held up a sweatshirt and remembered the day she had bought it at the five-and-dime. KETTLE CREEK was printed in bold letters across the front. Cynthia had been in the store with her mother that day, buying calico-print fabric. The sweatshirt would always remind her of how surprised Cynthia had been to see her teacher shopping in the same store, and how the sales clerk had told Cynthia to stop bothering the customer. The clerk's expression had hardened when she'd realized that Colleen wasn't bothered at all.

She repacked the Corningware and the blender in their original boxes. The tape recorder her father had mailed to her fit back into the Styrofoam mold. A shoebox could hold her father's tapes and the prerecorded music cassettes. Their collection had multiplied exponentially. The Post Exchange had the latest record albums for amazing prices. Colleen and Miguel now had more than fifty: the Rolling Stones, the Beatles, James Taylor, the Supremes, the Temptations, and more.

Colleen pulled the edge of a large envelope from between the album covers. Tears filled her eyes when she recognized that it contained the class picture taken when she was still at West Hill School. She had brought the school photos home before she knew they were closing the school.

She was drying her eyes with toilet paper in the bathroom when she heard someone knock. Colleen hurried to the front of the trailer, but no one was there by the time she opened the door. She could hear a voice calling, "Y'all in there? Hello . . . Hello . . ."

Leaning out the door, Colleen saw Jan banging on a window in the back bedroom. Jan was the last person she wanted to see.

"Hi, I'm over here. I was just packing up some things."

Jan rushed toward her. She waved a piece of paper and said, "Did you see this? It's outrageous."

"I don't know. Let me see."

Jan handed the paper to Colleen. A flyer announced that there would be a special meeting of the parish school board on Thursday at 6:00 p.m. in the cafeteria of Kettle Creek Elementary School.

"So, did you know about this?" Jan demanded.

Colleen handed back the flyer. "No. How did you find out?"

"My friend Rita told me. She works at your school."

"Rita Harper is your friend?" Colleen could feel her Irish temper rising.

"Yes, the colored parents requested a special board meeting because of the retentions. Didn't anyone at school tell you?"

"Rita Harper, the cop's wife, is your friend?" Colleen said it again, trying to make sense of it. *Birds of a feather . . .* She glared at Jan. "Nope, Rita doesn't talk to me. Looks right through me when we're in the same room. Not one of those white teachers gives me the time of day."

Shaking the paper, Jan told her, "Those uppity black folks don't want to accept that their youngins need more time to learn. Even your class isn't ready to move on, and they had a white teacher." Jan's mouth spewed those words as if she had eaten some rotten fruit. "Come on," she continued. "It's almost six o'clock. You can drive us there."

"Us? You want me to drive you?"

"Don't you think you should go? Find out if they retain them or pass them on? And they want to open up their school. I'm only trying to help you, darlin'."

Colleen resisted the desire to slap this fool of a woman. "Help me? You've done nothing but poison my days. The first thing you said when I got hired was that 'no decent white southern woman would take that job.' How was that helpful?"

"You don't understand how it is around here, that's all."

Colleen walked down the steps as she enunciated each syllable. "I understand exactly how it is here. People like you are filled with hate and fear because of the color of people's skin."

Jan shrank back, but her tone sharpened. "Only trying to give you some advice. I told you not to take the job Mrs. Kirby wouldn't. She said if she couldn't tell them apart, how would she ever learn their names? You acted like a Yankee from the start. That's why the white teachers don't tell you anything."

Colleen kept her rage at bay as she witnessed a retreat. She ached to avenge the pain this woman inflicted without a second thought. "A Yankee? This isn't about the North versus the South. This is about teaching children. I know every single one of their names." Colleen moved a step closer. "Cynthia has such delicate features. She'll be beautiful."

Jan stepped back.

"Linkston's tortoiseshell glasses magnify his deep brown eyes." Colleen took another step and leaned in. "Jarrod's ears stick out, and he squints. I think he needs glasses, but no one will listen to me. He's a tough one, but he's come around with respect and patience. Should I go on?"

Jan threw up her hands and squirmed away. Colleen stepped closer. "Plants need water, sunlight, and soil with room to grow. Students need good teachers, good books, and a good school. The board *should* open their school. That's where their roots are. Integrate *that* school."

The tables had turned. For the first time, Jan was speechless. In fact, she seemed frozen in place, unsure of what Colleen would do next.

Relief settled over Colleen as she realized that in two short weeks this woman would be out of her life. Was this the time to call upon that saying Jan had used so sweetly to twist a knife in her back? Yes. Colleen stepped back with a contented smile and took a deep breath to keep control.

"Bless your heart, Jan, you'll have to get someone else to take you. I do appreciate you coming by, but I have to finish packing." She heard the southern drawl come out of her own mouth, slow and sure.

Colleen shut the door and left Jan to stand alone in the heat of the humid Louisiana day. Then she did a little dance in the kitchen. However, her exuberance was short-lived as she wondered if she should go to the meeting. Was this meeting what Penelope Woods had meant when she'd said, "We're not done"? Would Cynthia's mother or grandfather be there? Mrs. Woods? Jan was partly right, again. Even now, Colleen didn't understand the unwritten rules about whom to talk to and how a misstep could put you in danger, as she had placed the children in danger by picking them up in her car. All she knew was that she didn't belong at the meeting. She went back to finish packing.

Chapter 45

●

Evelyn

Thursday, May 21, 1970

T he parish school board meeting was scheduled in the elementary school instead of the office building. The board was seated at the front of the room at cafeteria tables. Rows of chairs were set up for the public. A podium with a microphone had been placed to face the board. Evelyn had attended enough board meetings to recognize the typical arrangement, which allowed the public to speak or ask questions after the board president and other members gave their reports.

Looking around the room, she saw that all the seats were taken. Her stop to talk to Sissy—and probably her initial hesitation to attend the meeting—meant she would have to stand. Annie Mae was up front, flanked by Reverend Wilford and by Shelton's cousin Penelope Woods. The majority of the people at the meeting were black. The only white faces belonged to eight of the nine school board members; the police officers at the doors; white administrators from the high school; Mr. Palmer, the principal of the white high school; and his assistant principal, Mr. Armstrong. Besides the faithful board secretary, Bessie

Sanders, Mr. Peterson was the only Negro seated at the parish school board table.

As Evelyn looked at the crowd spilling into the hallway, she noticed Lulu Moberly, Annie Mae's friend Mavis, and Mrs. Wilson, the black school's secretary, standing together. Most of the people were still dressed for work.

The chatter in the room stopped as the board president, James Watson, started the meeting with a bang of his gavel. After the opening formalities, he stated that the purpose of this meeting was to explain the decision to delay the graduation of the students who had recently transferred to Kettle Creek High School.

"Ladies and gentlemen, our esteemed superintendent has suggested that I remind you of last October's communication from the Department of Health, Education, and Welfare, which accepted the desegregation plans of the Kettle Creek Schools as proposed by this school board:

"'Under explicit holdings of this court, the obligation of every school district is to terminate dual school systems at once and operate only unitary schools now and hereafter. It is our understanding that you closed West Hill High School and West Hill Elementary School, which previously operated under the Freedom of Choice plan and were predominately Negro schools.'"

Evelyn listened to the speaker review the events of the year, which had "resulted in total and complete desegregation, without any court battles." He touted the decision to move from "school choice" to "mandated closures" as having saved $1 million in federal funds.

The board president then introduced Cornelius Palmer to speak to the group. Palmer announced that the formally all-Negro West Hill High School would be converted to a vocational-technical school, and that there would be so many white pupils and teachers there that "we cannot even call it a Negro school anymore. More federal funds have been obtained, and now each school will be air-conditioned, so that teachers and students can take pride in their modern facilities."

Evelyn winced as she tried to see over several parents taller than she. Someone shouted from the back of the room. Heads turned.

"That's our school!"

Evelyn heard curses muttered through closed lips from people near her. Did the board really think this was satisfactory? Would no one acknowledge the community's pride and connection to that building? True, they had all kept their jobs, but most of the Negro teachers had become teachers' aides and lost their own classrooms. Maybe Evelyn had kept her class, but she didn't consider her air-conditioned portable classroom to fit the principal's view of "every penny in federal funds put to good use."

Lordy, those children had to wear sweaters all year long. They don't have air-conditioning at home. I'd rather have some new textbooks!

The restless stance of the parents around Evelyn worried her. How long would they all be able to listen to Palmer's smooth words?

Palmer continued by explaining his "generous offer" of a fifth year to the Negro high school seniors, to assure that they received a full curriculum before graduation. Evelyn held back a groan. He was so condescending. Would any attempt to question these decisions cut through the good old boys seated at the board table?

One hand went up at the front of the room. Evelyn recognized Penelope's manicured fingers and elegant wristwatch through the forest of parents in front of her. As Penelope rose, her towering height commanded the attention of the room. She was dressed in a white tailored pantsuit, and even though her Afro hairstyle was subdued with a white headband, it was not the smooth matron or pageboy style most of the black women of Kettle Creek sported. She waited to be recognized as the board members turned and whispered to one another. Finally, the board president explained that the question-and-answer period would begin when Mr. Palmer was finished with his remarks. He looked at Mr. Palmer.

"I'm finished," said the principal, surprising everyone.

The board president then announced that anyone wishing to speak could approach the microphone at the podium and needed to prove their residency in Kettle Creek by stating their name and address.

Penelope stepped up. The microphone only added to her command of the room.

The expression on some board members' faces gave them away.

Ha! You don't know who she is, do you? Evelyn thought.

"Good evening, and thank you for this opportunity to speak to you. My name is Penelope Woods. I'm a cousin of the late Shelton Woods and the granddaughter and namesake of the late Penelope Woods, from whom I inherited the farm on Woods Road, Kettle Creek, off Route 179. I own the farm and the horses that I raise there."

Evelyn saw the surprised looks. She knew that some of the board members recognized and remembered that the elder Penelope Woods had raised thirteen children and some grandchildren on that farm and that she had acquired that land from her ancestors who had been slaves there.

A police officer burst into the room then. His boots hit the floor with loud slaps as he rushed to the officers standing at the side doors near the board. One of them gestured to the board president, who then signaled the officer to come to the table.

Evelyn sensed that the interruption was about the students she had passed earlier. Sure enough, the board president told the assembly, "I've just been informed that a large group of students is seated on the lawn of the Negro high school and that they're planning to stay there until we let the seniors graduate."

The room was buzzing. The muttering became louder and clearer.

"What's wrong?"

"Kids at the high school?"

"Keep the police out of this!"

It took several minutes for the gavel to quiet the room.

Evelyn's courage returned when she saw that Penelope was still standing, waiting to speak.

The board president addressed the group with a second message. "Ladies and gentlemen, we have a situation that needs the immediate attention of our administrators. I believe we will need to postpone the remaining agenda items for another day."

He stood, ready to leave, but Penelope spoke up. "With all due respect, Mr. President, the majority of the people in this audience represent the students who are apparently sitting on the lawn. Why would this require the administrators' attention right now? Since I was invited to speak, I would like to do so. I *will* be brief."

The room started buzzing again. Shouts from the back of the room fueled the tension. "Let her speak!"

"We want to be heard tonight!"

"We've had enough!"

The two police officers at the doors moved forward toward the board members and the administrators still seated at the table, hands on their billy clubs. One appeared ready to grab his pistol. Visibly shaken, the white men at the front ducked their heads together, eyes lowered, as if they were afraid to look at the angry, shouting crowd.

The board president walked back to his place and sat down. Holding his hands above his head, he demanded quiet. He faced Penelope, but neither gave ground to the other. Evelyn wished she could catch Fred Peterson's eye at the front of the room. She knew he was smiling inside. Did it show? She could hear the collective thought as it hung over the community: *Who is this woman who won't back down?* Evelyn saw what the crowd saw: a fierce challenger, her mahogany black skin contrasting with her white clothing, her hair untamed.

The board president leaned over to talk to the superintendent of the parish schools. Shuffling through some paperwork, he pulled out a sheet and read, "I want to remind us all that because of the actions required to unify our schools, we did not lose millions of dollars of federal funds. We cannot restore the West Hill schools. We are mandated to integrate or lose that funding."

It was as if he were speaking only to Penelope. She responded directly to him. "Mr. President, we are here for only one reason tonight. The parents have asked me to speak for them. The parents of the seniors from West Hill High School do not accept the offer of the additional school year. Not one of those students was told that they were in danger of not graduating—not until they received a letter last week. Each of the seniors has completed the required courses from both the West Hill and Kettle Creek High Schools. Some of the seniors have already been accepted to colleges and plan to begin their higher education in September. By 'offering' a fifth year to assure a full curriculum, you appear to be admitting that the Kettle Creek School Board did not operate a 'separate but equal' educational facility for the schools that Negro students attended. We believe that we have the basis for a civil rights lawsuit, and our attorney is ready to file it tomorrow if the board does not reconsider its decision. However, if we can arrive at an agreement tonight, the administrators won't have to leave to decide what to do about the students sitting on the lawn of the only high school they knew until they were uprooted so abruptly this November."

The audience broke into loud applause. Shouts and whistles filled the room. Stunned, the board president sat down to speak to the board members closest to him at the table. After a few minutes of huddled whispers and nodding heads, he replied, "Miz Woods, are you threatening us? Are you certain you are speaking for all the seniors and their parents?"

Penelope drew herself up even more. Evelyn thought she would burst with pride at the woman's courage. "Sir," she said calmly, "I am *not* threatening you. I *am* speaking for all the seniors and their parents. I am stating the facts and offering a solution."

Chapter 46

ð

Frank

Thursday, May 21, 1970

F rank stared at Dedra. She was amazing. She listened to
the student who reported that a police car had just pulled
up behind the scrub pines next to the storage shed. The car had
crept down the main road with its headlights off, and two officers were now standing by its side.

Frank admired Dedra's commitment to the nonviolent plan.
When they couldn't enter the building, she sent a few as lookouts along the road leading to the campus. Then she directed
everyone to sit on the grassy area behind their old gymnasium.
Students passed whispered updates as they sat in a circle, arms
linked.

Frank saw them first. The two police officers walked over
to the students, billy clubs in their hands, pistols on their hips.
One held up a bullhorn and said, "Kettle Creek Police! You must
leave now!"

The students responded by chanting in unison, "Hell no, we
won't go!"

Chaos erupted. Surprised students helped each other off the

ground, stood up, linked arms, and created circles of tight bodies moving together, round and round.

"Hell no, we won't go!"

Their voices were strong, clear, firm.

"Hell no, we won't go!"

A second bullhorn from the rear of the school commanded, "You are trespassing! Go home or face arrest!"

The lookouts had missed another patrol car, parked on the opposite side of the building.

As the inner circle of football players and cheerleaders passed the outer circle, Frank saw his sister and her friends. He shouted, "Sissy, run home, now!"

He heard dogs barking as if they were tracking an animal. Breaking the line, he grabbed her. "You need to leave! Run through the path behind Miz Glover's house, get inside, and lock the door!"

"But Frank, we want to help too!"

He shook her shoulders hard. *"Now.* Take your friends."

As he watched Sissy, Pearl, and Kendra running away, he remembered the dog that had chased them on the first day of the crossover.

Dedra's voice rose above the others. "No. Quiet. Everyone sit down."

The inner circle of students stopped chanting and followed her command. Frank looked at their clenched jaws and pursed lips. No one made eye contact as they sat, still with linked arms, which protected them and kept them from running. The plan was to sit in silence as a form of passive resistance. Dedra had prepared them for taunts but not the dogs. Frank could smell the fear on his own body and the adrenaline rush that made him want to fight, not sit.

Frank felt his eyes widen as courage transformed his friend's face. Her expression hardened as she led them by example. Dedra had studied the sit-ins that university students held at lunch counters and had told them all about SNCC, the Student Nonviolent Coordinating Committee. They had all agreed that the school administration hadn't honored its promises to represent them on sports teams and student council. If they weren't going to be allowed to graduate, did any of it make sense? Frank couldn't help worrying. This wasn't 1957, they weren't the Little Rock Nine, and Dedra wasn't Rosa Parks. They didn't have organized support beyond themselves.

As Frank looked straight ahead, he saw the officers with the bullhorn. Two more officers had joined them, and they appeared to be arguing, but they were too far away to be audible.

Frank watched as a different man took the bullhorn. Low groans came from students near him. Frank felt his body tense and readied himself for bad news.

"Students, I am Captain Eastman. I've been sent to speak to you. Your parents are with the school board. They want to know what you're doing here. Can one or two of you speak with us?"

Frank looked at Dedra as she turned her head and broke the silence. "I can talk to you."

"What's your name, young lady?"

She remained seated and calmly said, "My name is Dedra. What we want is simple. We are going to sit here until the school board lets us graduate this year."

Chapter 47

❧

Evelyn

Thursday, May 21, 1970

Penelope finished her statement, and the whistles and applause subsided as she returned to her seat. A man stood at the front of the room to address the parish school board. From her standing-room-only position, Evelyn had to stretch onto her toes to see over the parents in front of her. She recognized the mayor and wondered what he would say this time. She suspected the worst. He was the one who had decided to close the playground in the center of town when he was directed to integrate it. When he had been challenged about that decision, he had reportedly answered, "Some folks think the mayor's council is a segregationist organization. Well, what's wrong with that?"

As Penelope gave up the microphone and walked back to her seat, Evelyn heard folks say, "Just like her grandmother." "She did us proud." "Those white folks didn't see it coming."

Waiting for the audience to quiet down, the mayor addressed the board with a casual yet direct manner. "Mighty good to see you folks on this fine night. May I suggest that a few of the esteemed parish school board members and our superintendent meet with Miz Woods and Reverend Wilford in my office across the street? I believe we can work this out. Kettle Creek's fine citizens are well represented here and will understand that we need to have a more private conversation."

The response from the crowd was instantaneous. Gasps and mutters exploded into shouted demands from angry parents.

"This is a public hearing!"

"No private meetings!"

"Stay right here!"

Evelyn had to peek through the shoulders and heads of the people in rows ahead of her. The mayor turned to see the entire room on its feet. For the first time, Evelyn saw fear on his face. Reverend Wilford was seated facing the mayor and must have seen his chance in the man's wide-eyed, slack-jawed expression. The reverend stood and turned to face the parents as he took command of the room.

"Parents, my good people, we are not in God's house tonight, but He is here with us. Please be seated. We will resolve our dispute here, not across the street."

Amid the parents' voices, the reverend's commands, and the gavel's banging, the parish school board president barked, "Order. Order. Order. Be seated or be escorted out of this meeting."

As the people settled down, he turned to the police at the front of the cafeteria and said, "Officers, escort anyone who disturbs this meeting out of the building immediately."

He then addressed the mayor, who was still standing at the microphone, "Mr. Mayor, with all due respect, I need to ask you to be seated as well. I will confer with the superintendent and the high school principal right here for a moment."

From her perch, Evelyn saw the three men standing in a

huddle behind the table. They called over one of the officers, who spoke with the school board president.

The hum of conversation and the sound of chair legs scraping the wood floor increased as the minutes ticked away. The crowd's patience was thinning. Evelyn's legs were tired, and her back ached. She checked her watch, surprised to see that only fifteen minutes had passed. She felt restless. She knew there were folks in the audience who wouldn't remain quiet much longer.

Finally, the parish school board president, the superintendent, and the principal took their places at the table. The board president looked around at the audience and said, "There are many strong positions here tonight. We are obligated to adhere to the legal ones. Our superintendent just reminded us that we would have lost our federal funding if we hadn't complied with the Supreme Court ruling. We cannot run a dual school system, or Freedom of Choice schools. We must unify the schools. As you know, the students are protesting our decision. Our police have surrounded the students at the Negro high school—"

A shout interrupted the president. "What do you mean, *surrounded*?"

"Let me continue. The students are quiet. The officer in charge is maintaining civil order among both the police and the students. We have instructed the chief to keep the situation nonviolent and to follow civil-disturbance guidelines: find the leaders; determine what they want and what their plan is. He reported that they are planning to sit there until we agree to let them graduate."

Another muffled shout came from the side: "They'll be sitting there till next May."

"Order. Order." The hammering of the gavel resonated throughout the room. "Do you want to stay? Order."

Evelyn looked at the faces of the parents she knew so well. She had taught many of their children, and she knew how important a good education was to all of them. The worried looks on their faces, their sweaty brows, the years of support they had given her overwhelmed her as she watched them fight for the right for the students to graduate on time.

"The decision to offer a fifth year to our seniors was generous. The offer is still available to those who would like to take it."

The same voice came from the side of the room: "You take it."

"Order. This is my last warning."

One of the officers moved over to the area where the voice had come from.

"If I am interrupted once more, the meeting will be terminated." The president looked over at the seated board and at the police, who nodded that they understood the command.

"Here is our decision. The superintendent has advised the board that we must acknowledge the coursework completed at West Hill High School and Kettle Creek High School and allow the seniors to graduate."

Sighs of relief were accompanied by cheers and clapping from the audience.

This time, the board president waited for silence without demanding it with his gavel.

"But we cannot agree to let them graduate from their high school building. It is closed. They must graduate from the Kettle Creek High School auditorium. West Hill High School will be noted on their diploma as the school they graduated from."

Evelyn saw through that compromise. The parish school board didn't want to claim the Negro students on its own diplomas. After all, they hadn't completed the "rigorous curriculum" of Kettle Creek High School. What about her third-graders? Would those retentions be rescinded as well?

The board president continued, "Parents, I do need a consensus. Please raise your hand if you agree with the board's decision to allow all students to graduate."

Evelyn raised her hand with everyone else in the room. Not everyone there was a parent. She wished that the white members of the school board understood that in the Negro community, *all* adults took responsibility for *all* their youngsters.

"It appears unanimous, but let me ask, does anyone disagree?"

Evelyn knew that the parents and the community had concerns but that no one would give up the agreement at this point. It was time to go home.

"Seeing no dissension, I call this meeting to a close. Good night."

Chapter 48

❧

Frank

Thursday, May 21, 1970

F rank was tired of sitting cross-legged on the grass. With his bulky body, he could never remain that way comfortably. With Dedra's arm linked with his, he was willing to sit there as long as it took, just to be close to her again, but they had been in this position for over an hour and he needed to shift his weight. As he did, he noticed some activity under the trees. Another patrol car pulled up to the group of police who had been standing there, watching them.

What for? We're just sitting here on the ground.

He recognized one as the cop who had arrested him. When he had walked over with the captain to talk to Dedra, Frank had seen the ropey scars on the man's arm. He remembered those scars. It was all he had been able to see when the cop had stepped on his back and grabbed Frank's arm to cuff his hands. His words were branded into Frank's memory: "Don't want no trouble from you, boy! Don't you be like your daddy, now!" Frank needed to find out the officer's name.

The captain interrupted Frank's contemplation when he

started speaking into the bullhorn: "Students, I have another message from the parish school board. The superintendent has recommended that you graduate this year. We now ask you to leave the school property and go home. Your parents are waiting for you."

Frank saw the surprised looks in each face. He expected shouts of victory, but they all looked to Dedra, who remained in place—no eye contact, no movement, no reaction. Not one student uttered a sound. No one moved. Frank leaned over to her. "Dedra? What's wrong? Shouldn't we leave?"

"Why should we trust them, Frank? They came out here with dogs and billy clubs. How do we know that what he said is true? It could just be a trick to make us go home."

Frank saw that the police remained in place as well. Maybe Dedra was right. Why weren't they leaving if it was over?

With the bullhorn still in his hand, the captain walked toward them, followed by the cop who had arrested him. When the captain was close to where Dedra and Frank were sitting, he called out to her. "Dedra, you kids got what you wanted. You need to leave."

Frank watched as she remained seated and looked up at the cops. The captain's left hand was on the bullhorn, but his right hand could grab the billy club or his pistol if he wanted to. Frank already knew how quickly the other officer could react. He readied himself to leap up.

"Officer, how do we know what you say is true?" Dedra asked.

Frank heard the exasperation in the captain's answer. "Look, I ordered the dogs to be put back into the cars. We've been out here with you for over an hour, waiting for the meeting that your parents asked for to be over. I'm telling you what they sent that patrol car out to tell me."

Dedra didn't blink. "If the meeting is over, then our parents will be coming to get us. We'll wait here for them."

As the two policemen walked away, Frank heard the one who had arrested him say, "Captain, you can't let that little bitch talk to you like that."

"Shut up, Beau. I'm following orders."

Chapter 49

🍎

Evelyn

Thursday, May 21, 1970

A s the meeting ended, Evelyn was finally able to get up to the front of the room to see how Annie Mae was doing. She needed to tell her that she had seen Sissy and her friends go to the high school. The tension in the room had turned to relief. Everyone was anxious to get home. Their high school seniors had been bold and brave, and now they probably thought they were invincible. Was that a good thing? Evelyn admired them and their effort, but she knew that the victory was also due to Penelope.

Annie Mae was at the edge of a rush of parents thanking Penelope for her words and support. Evelyn took her friend's hand before she realized that Annie Mae was dabbing at tears rolling down her cheeks.

"Evelyn, you're here. I didn't see you. I was worried that you hadn't come."

"I have something to tell you. I left late, and on my way here I saw Sissy, Pearl, and Kendra walking toward the high school with blankets and food."

"What? Those girls. I should have known they were up to

something. And Frank? Did you see him? Oh, Lordy. Are they all at the high school? Of course they are—I can feel it in my bones. I need to go home."

"I can take you, or do you need to go with the reverend and Penelope?"

"No, no, please take me, Evelyn. It's out of their way for them to take me back."

As Evelyn and Annie Mae drove up to the high school, they saw police cars parked along the road. Evelyn drove around the back of the school, where she had seen the students gathering. They both gasped at the sight of more than seventy students sitting on the grass in a circle with their arms linked together. Behind them, by the trees and the fence that bordered the school property, were more police cars and about six officers standing and watching the seated students.

As they got out of the car, Evelyn said, "Annie Mae, what do we do?"

"Looks like we don't have to figure that out. Look who's coming."

A lone figure walked toward them, his stride confident, a bullhorn in his hand, his billy club swinging.

"Good evening, missus. I'm Captain Eastman. Do you know any of these students?"

"Good evening, Captain. I'm Annie Mae Woods, and this is my friend Evelyn Glover. My son and daughter might be here. We're coming from the parish school board meeting."

Evelyn sensed some relief in the man's expression as he said, "Good—then you're aware of the decision to let the students graduate on time? These kids didn't trust us, wanted to wait for their parents to tell them. I told them, but they won't leave."

While they talked, a few more cars passed the school. Evelyn noticed one turn back instead of going into the unpaved road leading to their community.

"Annie Mae, look—some of the others saw us. They're coming back."

Captain Eastman turned to see the cars arriving. Evelyn saw him slip his hand around his belt to move the billy club to his back.

"If you ladies could come with me so the students can see you while I tell them again that they can graduate next week and that it's time to go home, we would appreciate it."

Evelyn looked wide-eyed at Annie Mae as she thought, *A white man is telling me he would appreciate it?*

They followed Captain Eastman, who raised the bullhorn to speak at the same time that a few more parents walked toward them.

"Students, I believe you know these women, Missus Woods and Missus Glover. They just left the meeting that I told you about. They agree that you can go home and that you will graduate."

Evelyn and Annie Mae nodded their heads. Evelyn scanned the group of students and spotted Frank and Dedra but not Sissy and her friends.

"There's Frank, Annie Mae. He's coming over."

The students gathered their blankets and sacks of food quietly. Evelyn stepped back as Frank greeted his mother. "Ma. Don't be upset. I'm fine."

"Where is your sister? Miz Glover told me that Sissy was here too."

"When the police started to arrive, I told her to go home by the path behind Miz Glover's house. She's safe. Nothing has happened since that captain got here."

Evelyn gave Annie Mae a worried look. *Since he got here? What happened before?*

"Frank, I'm driving your mother home. Come with us to find Sissy."

The captain was on the bullhorn again, this time with more force and less patience. "You are trespassing on public property. You all need to leave now."

As Evelyn drove away with Annie Mae and Frank, she doubted that any of those white officers had ever worried before about protecting their black school, now their "public property."

Chapter 50

◈

Evelyn

Friday, May 22, 1970

The next day, Evelyn sat in Annie Mae's living room while she waited for her friend to bring her a cup of tea. She didn't want to be waited on and would have preferred to stay in the kitchen, but Annie Mae had scooted her out. Evelyn chose the chair by the large window. The woodwork was stained a dark mahogany to match the best pieces of furniture in the room. The tufted "ladies'" chair was upholstered in a wine-colored damask. In the kitchen, Annie Mae was talking to Rachel, her second-grader, who was in Colleen's class. Now that the high school graduation problem was resolved, what could be done about the elementary students?

Annie Mae carried the tea and some shortbread cookies into the room. She would never have let her children eat in here, but Evelyn knew she loved serving friends in her "best" room.

The back door slammed shut, echoing through the hall between the kitchen and the living room. "Ma, I'm home."

Annie Mae called to her son, "Frank, come greet our company in the living room."

Evelyn admired the way Annie Mae tutored her children with manners—gently but with high expectations.

"Hello, Frank. I haven't seen you since I drove you and your mother home last night."

"Yes, ma'am. Thank you for the ride."

"How's your job at the funeral home?"

"It's been great. I really like being able to drive the hearse. Miz Glover, I'm glad to see you. I have a question. Did you see the cop who was standing with the captain when you arrived? Do you know his name?"

Evelyn caught Annie Mae's eye. She looked worried.

"I'm not sure of it, Frank, but I think he owns that auto repair shop at the end of Highway 179. Why do you ask?"

"He just always seems to be around, watching me driving. His first name is Beau."

Evelyn heard Annie Mae catch her teacup as it hit the saucer a bit too hard.

She looked at her son and said, "Frank, why are you asking about him? He's the one who arrested you back in November. I saw his name on the paperwork when I signed you out."

"Ma, did you see his last name?"

"Yes, it's Harper. Are you in trouble with him?"

"No. He's just always around, that's all. I just wanted to know."

Chapter 51

❦

Frank

Friday, May 22, 1970

Frank went into his bedroom and sat down on the bed to open the envelope he had taken from the mailbox. He didn't like keeping secrets from his mother. He had to decide how to tell her. The prior November, when he'd turned eighteen, he'd had to register for the draft. She knew that, but not that he had received a form to report his plans for after his graduation. He was classified as 1-S since he was still a high school student.

Frank had ignored the college application process because without a scholarship he didn't have the money, and he didn't qualify for a deferment without a college acceptance. As required, he had notified Selective Service of the change in his status as a student. The job at the funeral home had given him some hope; however, it just wasn't enough. Sure, he still had the summer to work and could enroll somewhere in September, but that was his old thinking. And the past week had brought changes he hadn't planned on. He was ready to move on with his future and whatever it brought.

So, in a week, as of Friday, May 29, 1970, he would be a high school graduate with a 1-A classification and could be drafted into military service. He didn't have to open the envelope; he knew this was his new card. Now he was certain he knew who had started the fire that his father had died in. It wasn't an accident. It was murder. His father's repair shop had been a threat to the "best mechanic in West Louisiana." The scars on Beau's arm were burns.

Frank took the lighter from his pocket and looked at the engraved initials, BNH. What was Harper's middle name? Did it matter? What could he do about it? Could one eighteen-year-old make a difference?

Yes. He knew three men who'd enlisted together at eighteen, all three marines: his father, Ole Man Everett, and Fred Peterson. They had returned to Kettle Creek after Korea, and each had made a difference in his own way. His father had been a devoted family man who held a job, started a business, and was a leader in the local NAACP. Fred Peterson had gone to college on the GI Bill and come back to a career in education. Ole Man Everett struggled with nightmares from combat but used his tracking skills to hunt in the woods and alert his neighbors to suspicious activity.

What could Frank do? He still had the business card the FBI agent had given his mother four years earlier. The office's address was in a large city about ninety miles away. He could write a letter to the agent explaining that he had found the lighter next to his father's shoe on the night of the fire and had kept it secret all this time, but that would put his family at risk. He couldn't do that. He put the lighter in his pocket.

Frank drove to the army base and asked to speak to Sergeant Barry, the recruiter who had come to his school. He didn't have to wait long. Sergeant Barry greeted him and walked him back through the recruiting headquarters, a rabbit warren of cramped offices.

"It's good to see you again. I remember you from Kettle Creek High School; you had questions about college benefits. Weren't you a football player? Frank's your name, isn't it?"

"Yes, I'm Frank Woods, and I was a football player. But that's over. I wanted to ask you more about enlisting. I'm 1-A, and I don't want to wait to get drafted."

"If you enlist, you serve three years active duty and three years inactive reserve. A draftee serves two years active duty."

"My father worked in the motor pool. Is there a way I could enlist and have that assignment?"

"You want to work with your father, on this base?"

"No, he passed a few years ago. He was a civilian worker."

"You know your way around cars, Frank?"

His mind flashed back to the day he had been under his mother's old car with oil dripping in his eye. Changing the oil in her car that day had been the last thing he'd wanted to do, but it had given him a sense of pride. And driving the hearse for the funeral home required him to step up and recall all the things his father had taught him about cars. He hadn't realized how much he knew until he tried to impress Mr. Fields.

"Enlisting can allow a guaranteed MOS if you qualify for it."

"MOS?"

"Oh, sorry, MOS stands for 'military occupational specialty.' Tell me a bit more about yourself. Did you graduate from high school?"

Frank thought about how that almost hadn't happened. "Yes, sir. Well, almost—we graduate next Friday."

"Enlisting in the army was a great career choice for me, Frank. What else are you interested in?"

"Football."

"Yes, I see that you're in good shape. I guess that's from training and practice. But we don't do much football. We have some windmill baseball competitions in the spring, but those are for soldiers here on a permanent assignment. Anything else?"

Frank put his hand into his pocket and felt the coolness of the lighter.

"Law enforcement, maybe military police?"

Sergeant Barry reached into his desk and took out a folder. "How 'bout I give you this brochure and some paperwork for you to look over? You said you're expecting a draft notice. If you enlist before that happens, you'll have more control over what your assignment will be because we'll be looking at you as a possible career candidate. You can specify what MOS or training you want as long as you qualify and don't screw up. You can also specify where you want to go before you enlist. As long as a position is open, you'll be guaranteed a one-year assignment there. After that, you go where the army needs you."

Frank took the folder. He'd talk it over with his mother, but he was ready to sign up. He might wind up in Vietnam, but not everyone did. Enlisting promised to give him some choices. And someday he would find a way to avenge his father's murder.

Chapter 52

Frank

Tuesday, May 26, 1970

The conversation with his mother hadn't gone well. Frank had explained his plan to enlist in the army, but she met it with more concern and resistance than he had expected. Without a full-time college acceptance, he was almost guaranteed to be drafted before the year was over, and of course she was worried he'd be sent to Vietnam.

Frank had argued that if he enlisted he'd have a better chance of controlling his assignment, at least for the first year, but there was no convincing his mother. Distraught, she called Miss Glover and invited her over to talk with them on Sunday afternoon. Why couldn't his mother let him decide? He knew Miss Glover was a good friend to them both. She had guided him to get the job at the funeral home.

At exactly 1:00 p.m. on Sunday, Miss Glover had rung the bell at the front door. "Frank, go on and invite Evelyn into the parlor. I'll be right there," his mother said. It was a ploy. Miss Glover didn't need an invitation, and why had she come to the front door? She usually knocked at the back, called to his mother, and came inside.

Frank knew he had been trapped, so he just sat and listened. It was Miss Glover's idea to talk to Mr. Peterson before he signed any paperwork. Frank wasn't happy about that. He had avoided speaking to the principal since the day he'd fixed the oil leak under his mother's car. He had finally agreed to meet with Mr. Peterson only to stop his mother's and Miss Glover's questions. Those two women had been unrelenting. Frank ended the inquisition with a promise to go to Mr. Peterson's office after school on Tuesday, since school was closed on Monday for Memorial Day.

It was 4:00 p.m. when Frank arrived at the office unannounced. The longer he delayed, the fewer people would be around. It was quiet, but Millie, the main secretary, was still there.

"Is Mr. Peterson here?" Frank asked.

Her eyebrows rose, and she faked a smile. "He's busy. Needs to redo the entire graduation list. I'm waiting to type it. I don't know if he has time to see you."

Frank swallowed the words he wanted to say and asked, "Could you please tell him that Frank Woods would like to speak with him?"

Before she could rise, Mr. Peterson opened his door with a pad of paper in his hand. "Hello, Frank. Did I hear you ask to see me?" He stepped back into his office and gestured with his free hand. "Come in." He closed the door behind them.

Frank wished his father were alive, for many reasons. As he avoided eye contact and looked down at Mr. Peterson's polished shoes, his father's shoe flashed behind his eyes. The memory of having found his father's shoe ripped open the pain he had buried and brought his anger back to the surface. The small office closed in on him. He needed air. He wanted to open the door, but then that secretary would hear their conversation. He pushed down the feelings.

"Are you all right, Frank?" Mr. Peterson asked.

Frank jammed his hands into his front pockets and nodded. "My mama and Miz Glover asked me to talk to you."

Mr. Peterson leaned back in his chair. "I know. Miz Glover filled me in. Let's go somewhere else." He glanced toward the secretary sitting in the main office, then picked up the pad of paper from his desk and led the way out. "Millie, here's the completed list. I'm finished for today. Have a good evening."

They walked around the school, toward the football field. Frank was surprised to notice that he was a bit taller than Mr. Peterson. It made him feel more equal and filled him with confidence. Small talk about end-of-year graduation plans quelled the awkwardness of the walk. Mr. Peterson had always been fair with him. Maybe this would help.

They sat down on the lower bleachers, and the principal cut to the purpose of the conversation: "You know your mama doesn't want you to enlist in the army. Can we talk about your reasons?"

"She doesn't understand. I expect that you do. Can't you see that I want to control my own life? I've been living under the shadow of my father's death. I need to move out from it."

Sorrow clouded the features of the older man's face.

"Mr. Peterson, I have a question before I answer yours. Why did you bring the FBI into our house four years ago?"

The principal's look of sorrow changed to one of surprise, and his usual baritone softened when he said, "Because what happened to your father was not an accident, and the NAACP came to me for help to prove it."

Frank remembered how scared he had been standing in the doorway, watching the government agents and his mother. "What did they know?"

Mr. Peterson leaned forward and answered, "They had suspicions but no proof."

Four years earlier, Frank had felt as if he couldn't do anything. Now he could. Now he wanted information that he had only been able to guess at from listening in on his mother's conversations. "What suspicions did they have?" he asked.

Mr. Peterson shifted on the bleacher. He leaned in closer to look into Frank's eyes and pursed his lips. Frank started to sweat in anticipation. Mr. Peterson finally spoke. "First, there was a pattern of injuries at Armstrong Rubber Company after the cafeteria, bathrooms, and drinking fountains were desegregated. The Natchez NAACP claimed that the plant was 'infested with Ku Klux Klansmen.'"

Frank took in this information with a deep breath to slow his racing heart. He looked away, not sure he wanted to hear more.

A vein popped out in Mr. Peterson's neck as he continued, "I knew some of these men from our service in the Korean War. A lot of vets had been hired, and they were involved in making some changes. We had more equal treatment in service than we did when we returned. I think I told you how hard it was to come home to a country that didn't respect our service."

"So, how did the FBI get involved with my father's death?"

"Right before your father died, there was a truck explosion near the plant. A bomb blew the truck apart and killed the driver instantly. That driver was on his way home from his work shift. Your father had worked with that man before he got the job on the base. Even the governor called it murder. They asked me to help."

"Why you?" Frank asked.

"The FBI came to me and Reverend Wilford. We know the community. We knew the men who worked with your daddy when he was at Armstrong."

Frank pivoted on the bench, as a force exploded from deep inside him, to face the meaning of the message hanging in the air between them.

"My mama told me about that man. She was worried. You were working with the FBI? They suspected the Klan? Does my mama know that? You knew this all these years and never told me?"

Mr. Peterson held his place and let Frank's anger spill over him.

"You put our family in danger by bringing the FBI into our house."

No longer able to stay seated, Frank leaped up and kicked the fence so hard that the chain link sagged.

"You know how afraid we all were right after he died."

Now Frank paced up and down the path between the field and the bleachers. "Hey, man, don't you have anything to say to me? I trusted you; my mama trusted you. We all did. You betrayed us." His heart thumped as hard as it did when he was running for a pass with no thought except to catch the ball.

Mr. Peterson leaned forward and gripped the plank of the bleacher he was seated on. "I never betrayed you, Frank, or your father. For four years, I've kept my promise to your daddy, and to my friend."

"What promise?" Frank's chest rose and fell with rapid breaths as he waited for an answer.

Peterson stood to answer Frank's question. "To protect you and to find the man who started the fire."

Frank stopped pacing. "When did you make that promise?"

Peterson sat back on the bench and rubbed his temples, as if to pull the memory out. "The night he died, I was there. I helped carry him to the truck and took him to the army base hospital. He could hardly speak, but he managed to tell me it wasn't an accident—it was arson." He looked up at Frank.

Frank couldn't breathe, couldn't talk. He felt empty. He nodded in agreement and sat on the bench next to Mr. Peterson. After a moment, he asked, "Anything else?"

Mr. Peterson put a trembling hand on Frank's shoulder as he spoke. "He had closed up shop to go home. He saw flames and someone running away. He shouted at the runner but ran back to the garage to try to put out the fire. His clothes caught. He rolled out. He knew you were coming with his supper. He wanted to know if you were okay."

Guilt, sorrow, and memories raced around in Frank's mind. His father had worried about him as he lay burning on the ground. "I found him. I called for help."

"He knew."

Frank couldn't hold back his sobs. "How? Why?"

"Your father asked me to protect you. I tried to tell you after you got arrested. The local police said the fire in your father's shop was an accident. That was the end of it until the FBI launched investigations into any deaths similar to the truck explosion in Natchez. They're still investigating. They contact me every year around the anniversary of the fire, but they need proof to bring charges."

Frank wiped off his face with his sleeve and reached into his pocket. "I have proof." He handed the lighter to Mr. Peterson and told him how he had found it next to his father's shoe and then hid it in his room.

Mr. Peterson took in a sharp breath of disbelief as he stared at the lighter in his hand. "Why didn't you tell me?"

"I was scared. Scared for my mother and for my sisters and my little brother."

Peterson looked at the engraving on the lighter. "I see. I know who this belongs to. This is a rogue cop. His chief has trouble with him."

Frank said, "I heard the chief telling him to shut up when we were sitting on the grass."

The older man continued, "I've been watching you. You kept your promise to me and stayed out of trouble. This is important evidence. Can I give it to the agent who has been in touch with me?"

Frank nodded in silent agreement. He breathed in the fresh air of freedom as he exhaled the secret. He realized he hadn't trusted anyone since his football coach had left and his school had closed. But he was still afraid for his mother, he realized, pressing his lips together.

As if Mr. Peterson were reading his thoughts, he said, "You were right to be worried for your family, Frank. Don't be so hard on yourself—you were only a boy. The FBI will be the best way to handle this."

"I'm still worried. Can the FBI really protect my mama?" Frank said.

"Things are changing in our town. Some people, like the police chief and the school superintendent, are speaking up. It's not just the FBI that will protect you and your family."

Frank relaxed a bit. "Maybe. You mean, like my father's cousin Penelope convincing them to let us graduate?"

"Yes, she sure surprised all of us. Didn't forget her roots. Smart one, that Penelope. But it took the laws and her courage to speak up." Mr. Peterson stood. "Let's walk some more. Don't we have to talk about your plan?"

After walking around the football field twice, the two men had an agreement: Mr. Peterson would take the lighter to the agent, and Frank would enlist, as he wanted to, after he told his mother the whole story.

Chapter 53

🍎

Colleen

Friday, May 29, 1970

It was the last day of the school year. The playground was filled with appropriate glee when the students spilled out of the classrooms. But all Colleen could think was, *They should be moving on to third grade.* She wished the parents knew that she believed in their children and had argued for them to be promoted. She was still invisible, not welcome. The Teacher Appreciation Luncheon had proven it. There was still no place for her at the lunch table. The only difference was that a couple of embarrassed PTA ladies had set up extra places when the unplanned-for teachers from the temporary trailer classrooms arrived.

Colleen was packing up her personal teaching supplies. She started to shove the thick black leather belt to the back of the desk drawer but changed her mind and tossed it into the trash bin. *I should have done that my first day.*

The door opened, interrupting her melancholy mood, and Evelyn came in.

"Hi," Colleen said. "That luncheon reminded me of the first time I had lunch in this school. I couldn't eat. My stomach was in knots. They were so surprised when we walked in. We never did get an invitation."

"Which was exactly why we went. We belonged there."

Colleen smiled sadly.

"Why that face?" Evelyn asked.

"Sorry. Look at Cynthia's column." Colleen unrolled the book incentive chart. "She learned to love books. This proves it. I should be happy about that."

Colleen pointed to the small box lying on the desktop. "I don't know what to do with my gift." When they had walked in, one of the PTA mothers had left the luncheon and come back minutes later with a bag from McCory's five-and-dime.

"Did they think we wouldn't notice that the white classroom teachers got handheld tortoiseshell mirrors and we got purse-size metal-framed ones?" Anger flooded Colleen's body. How could those women treat them so poorly?

Evelyn took the mirror from the box and held it up, pretending to admire herself. "Did you hear what you just said? Look in this mirror, Colleen. You're white, remember?" She put the mirror away and handed it back to Colleen, along with a flat package wrapped in brown paper. "I'm going to keep mine forever to remember how they tried to forget about us but we didn't let them."

"What's this?" Colleen asked.

"Just open it."

Colleen took off the brown paper sleeve, and a magazine slipped out. "*Instructor* magazine. Thank you, Evelyn—how thoughtful. I'm embarrassed to say I didn't get a gift for you."

"You offered me your carpet pieces. I'm here to claim them. And I didn't know about this magazine. This month's issue has an article that you might be able to use someday."

"What? Where?" Colleen flipped through the pages.

"Later. Not now." Tugging at her pearls, Evelyn looked away.

"Thank you again," Colleen said. "And there's something I've never told you. You remind me a bit of my mother."

A bewildered look filled Evelyn's face. "How could I remind you of your mother?"

"It was that cake you made me—my favorite lemon-flavored cake with fluffy lemon icing to match—and your pearls. Pearls were my mother's fashion statement."

Tears filled Evelyn's eyes.

"What's wrong? It was a compliment. Why are you upset?" Colleen asked.

Evelyn's voice trembled as she said, "I've been transferred."

"What are you talking about? Why?"

"I never sent the letters home to my students. Insubordination. Almost cost me my job. A transfer was their final concession. The parish school board felt it had compromised enough letting the seniors graduate."

Colleen was silent at first. Then she blurted out, "How do you stand this? I've barely managed a single year."

"We count on each other. I'd be lost without Annie Mae, Lulu, and Mavis."

A knock on the trailer door surprised Colleen. Evelyn opened it to let a young man enter. Colleen recognized Frank immediately. His sister Rachel was one of her students.

"Frank, this is Miz Rodriguez."

He greeted Colleen with a nod. "Pleased to meet you, ma'am."

"I remember you, Frank. We met once before. It was the first day we came to this school. You walked your sister to my line." Colleen looked toward Evelyn for a clue about why he was there.

"I was just telling Miz Rodriguez how much I count on my

friends." She threw her hands into the air in a welcome gesture. Turning to Colleen, she said, "You asked how I do it. This is how. Frank came to help me take my personal belongings home from my classroom. I asked him to come help me carry the carpet pieces you offered me. I can take them to my new school."

"I was going to help you carry them to your classroom." Colleen walked over to move them off the desk they were stacked on.

"Frank can take care of that. He's a strong young man, graduating tonight and enlisted in the army yesterday."

Frank easily picked up the carpet pieces that Colleen was struggling with. "Let me take them, Miz Rodriguez." He turned to leave, balancing the stack as he opened the door.

After a bit of hesitation, Colleen added, "Please tell your mother I said hello and thank you. She helped me convince the parents to sign permission slips for the library cards."

"Yes, ma'am. I'll give my mother the message." He nodded to Evelyn—"I'll put these in your car"—and left.

Evelyn asked, "What will you do when you go home to New Jersey?"

Colleen stared blindly at the *Instructor* magazine Evelyn had given her. Then she looked up to answer.

"I'm lucky—I have a choice. The inner-city school I resigned from has some openings. It's been hard to keep teachers since the riots in Newark."

"Inner city? Black schools?"

"No, it's an integrated school, and I can probably have my old classroom back. My replacement didn't stay."

"So, what's the choice?"

"I've also been offered a job in my hometown. Fourth grade. I turned it down two years ago to work in the city school."

"Two jobs? Seems like you'll do fine." Evelyn's eyes sparkled as she added, "Maybe you can take some kids to the library."

Colleen felt her mouth curve into a smile at the bit of humor. She took a risk and hugged her proud and prickly friend.

Miguel added a duffel bag to the three suitcases already in the trunk. The boxes of housewares, linens, and clothes and the stereo system she had packed were gone, shipped to her parents' house, courtesy of the US Army. Sitting on the backseat was a cooler packed with sandwiches, snacks, and drinks for the trip. Not everything they owned.

Colleen watched Miguel settle into the driver's seat. The dawn sun gently filtered through the trees behind the trailer. An early start could get them halfway to New Jersey. His two years of enlisted service were over. Her school year was done. Jarrod, Rachel, Cynthia, and Linkston had been her students, yet she had learned more from them than she could ever have imagined. Their parents and the other teachers, especially Evelyn, had made a lasting impression on her. But so had Rita's and Jan's vindictive actions.

Miguel leaned over the console to kiss her. "Ready? Let's go home."

She nodded, too full of emotion to speak.

Epilogue

🍎

Colleen

Thursday, November 5, 1970

Six months later, Colleen walked into school, anxious about that day's lesson. It was the one-year anniversary of the overnight closure to force public school integration in the small town she had taught in. Memories flooded her mind. On their last day together, Evelyn had given her the latest copy of *Instructor* magazine, a trusted resource they had used. One article included an exercise written by Jane Elliott, with objectives and activities. After Martin Luther King was shot, a dismayed Elliott had developed the exercise, based on eye color, to teach her students about discrimination. Lessons learned from the year in Louisiana wouldn't lie quietly for Colleen. Evelyn had known her better than she had realized.

Colleen organized things on her desk, making sure that the shades were exactly even with each other, because if the principal passed by and they weren't lined up properly, he would come in and fix them. She didn't want him to have a reason to do that today. He'd have questions. Would he like her answers?

At exactly 8:35 a.m., the bell rang and the students entered the school.

"Good morning, chickadees!" Colleen said, as she opened the door to a line of smiling faces.

As the students started to take the seats that they had used since school started in September, she made an announcement. "Boys and girls, please put your coats on the hooks, but don't sit until everyone is here."

Excited chatter spilled into the room.

"Mrs. Rodriguez, what are we doing today? I can help." Emily was a precocious child. It was hard to stay one step ahead of her.

Colleen stood straighter, with her shoulders thrown back. She knew she was taking a risk, but she started to explain the exercise in a more formal tone than she typically used. "If you have blue eyes, please sit in the three rows near the windows."

Emily's blond braids swung wide as she whipped her head around to find her friend Maddy.

"If you have brown eyes, please sit in the three rows closer to the door."

Emily's hand shot up, but her words wouldn't wait for permission to speak. "Maddy and I always sit together. I have blue eyes; she has brown."

"I know, Emily, but it's just for today. Can you do what I asked, please?"

Confused expressions washed over their faces, but the children obeyed her. Some looked into each other's eyes, as if to check that they were walking in the right direction.

During the few minutes while the children moved into different seats, Colleen hesitated and almost changed her mind. The weight of possible consequences held her back for a moment. This was an all-white community. She knew the town well but didn't understand the history behind its lack of diversity. She counted on her strong reputation as a valuable addition. She had worked for the district each summer during college and had done her student teaching there.

There were a lot of brown-eyed children in her class this year, but not one brown face looked back at her. Then she thought of Jarrod, Rachel, Cynthia, and Linkston. She owed them something. They would never know, but she would.

"Children, today we're going to see what it's like to feel different. We're going to do an experiment." A few of the students perked up at the word *experiment*.

"So, for this morning, if you have blue eyes, you will have to be patient with the brown-eyed children, because they're not as smart as you are."

Emily's hand shot up again, but Colleen ignored it. Of course the girl wanted to defend her best friend, but Colleen couldn't allow any discussion. Not yet. That would come at the end of the day. She plowed through the script printed in the magazine. The night before, she had practiced saying the words aloud so that she wouldn't choke on them.

"It's a fact. Blue-eyed people are smarter than brown-eyed people. This morning, only blue-eyed people can use the water fountain. Brown-eyed people will have to use cups."

Children covered their eyes. "Blue-eyed children may get library books at snack time. Brown-eyed children may not."

Heads shook in disbelief. Mouths gaped in surprise.

"Blue-eyed people will get five extra minutes at recess because they are better. Brown-eyed children may not play with blue-eyed children."

Emily put her head down on her desk.

"Blue-eyed people go to lunch first. Brown-eyed people will stand at the end of the line. I'll explain the rules if you forget."

Colleen held her head high and took a deep breath for courage. "Now, let's begin our day. Please stand for the Pledge of Allegiance."

Twenty-six pairs of eyes rounded in surprise. It would be a very long day. Could she really do it? Her decision to try the Jane Elliott experience with the children was challenging in more ways than one.

It was a professional risk for a new teacher to try something so controversial. The bile had risen from her gut as she'd recited the script. Were her words covered in the repulsion she felt?

It was also a personal risk. Would she fail? It had not been an easy lesson for her to learn. Not only had she gained new perspectives during the school year in Louisiana, she had also acquired new knowledge of her country—and of herself. She had a responsibility to share that insight.

Author's Note

What are the *Freedom Lessons?*

1. Treat others as you would like to be treated.
2. Have courage to confront uncertainty, intimidation or danger.
3. Family provides security, identity and values.
4. Prejudice is taught and learned.
5. It takes individual actions to create social change.

Unapologetically, I am a white woman who has written a book about school desegregation in the Deep South during the school year of 1969-1970 from three points of view: a white woman's, a black youth's, and a black woman's. How could I? Why did I do this? Because I had a story to tell. I wasn't sure whom it was for. Initially, it was to be a memoir about my own experience that year, for my daughters and my grandchildren. It became a novel, a fictionalized version of a mandated, unplanned, overnight integration of public schools. As I started to write the memoir version forty years later, I realized that some parts were missing. I wondered how this same event played out in the lives of the teachers and students I knew at the time.

When I started to research the background of the era that I thought I knew, it became clearer that I knew only my version. With the help of my local librarian, I found and read Gary

Clarke, EdD's, doctoral dissertation, *Even the Books Were Separate*. It documented the history and emotional impact of, decisions surrounding, resistance to, and life lessons he learned through first-person interviews about that school year. I am most grateful for his permission to use information and phrases from his dissertation, "Even the Books Were Separate: Court-Mandated Desegregation and Educators' Professional Lives During the Caddo Crossover of 1969-70. Copyright 2006 by Gary Lee Clarke. Reading his work was the first validation of my experience after forty years. Gary was a high school student during the school year 1969–70, when I was a teacher. That year impacted many decisions, particularly career choices, for the remainder of my life. Gary is now a retired school adminis-trator and also served as one of my beta readers.

If any reviewers look at this story through the #ownvoices lens, it won't pass. But I didn't write this story for black women or black men, although I hope they read it. I wrote it mainly for white women and white men because in my research I learned things about black history, culture, and families that I never knew. How didn't I know? When I was a student, these lessons were never taught to us—I had to experience them firsthand. I am open to, curious about, and interested in other cultures. I always have been. I married a Cuban man at a time in our country's history when our marriage was frowned upon by some and caused some concern in my own family. However, our union has flourished for fifty years. One of our daughters is married to a black man. I attribute the fact that she fell in love with someone from another race and culture to the way we raised our daughters and our continued interest in people from all walks of life. When my husband and I married, our daughter's mar-riage would have been illegal in nearby states. There are books and a movie, *The Loving Story,* that document that truth. I hope that my novel will generate conversations that are necessary in today's world.

This fifty-year-old story is a reflection of today's political climate. Unfortunately, many US schools are still segregated, for a variety of reasons. A few still resist the Supreme Court's 1954 *Brown v. Board of Education* decision and the Civil Rights Act of 1964. Discrimination, prejudice, and numerous examples of social injustice remain. Initial interest in reading my book came from readers of historical fiction and social justice stories and for professional development in the realm of discrimination.

The period from June 1969 to November 1970 documents actual events, some that I experienced and attributed to fictional Colleen. The final scene of the book was based on a lesson plan published in an *Instructor* magazine that I owned at the time. I credit Jane Elliott, the teacher who originally used the lesson in her own classroom the year Martin Luther King Jr. was murdered. However, I would not advise any teacher today to use that lesson in a class of young children. Lessons on discrimination and racial bias should be part of the general curriculum, and teachers should receive professional development on these issues.

When I started to write this book, I wished I'd had a friend to guide me that year, so I created her and named her Evelyn, in honor of a black woman I do call a friend, Evelyn Counts. My real-life Evelyn has always been a kind woman. Frank's devotion to his family and his loving respect for his mother are based on two men I know well: my husband, Manny, raised in the Cuban culture, and my son-in-law Philip, raised in the Ghanaian culture. If I needed to know how Frank would act in a situation, I channeled one of them. The intersections of Evelyn's and Frank's stories with my story are fictionalized versions of factual events that occurred in nearby cities and states during the same year.

This isn't a white-savior story, nor can I claim to have written a novel of diversity. As a white woman writing in the voice of a young black male and a black woman, I expect some pushback on how I could have done that.

This is how: I asked two black readers to read with a critical eye. I added two white beta readers, who wrote and published similar books representing black voices. Gary's dissertation and two others gave me firsthand accounts by teachers and high school students, as did newspapers of the day.

I also went back to the school and met the current principal, who was a college freshman during that year. Her brother was one of the black students who was to be held back and not graduate. The scenes in which Penelope argues for the students to be allowed to graduate are entirely fictional but based on a first-person interview reporting that parents did demand that the graduation take place. I have taken care in telling my point-of-view characters' stories in a respectful manner. I am also an experienced (retired) educator and have worked in segregated and integrated school systems as a teacher, a consultant, and a supervisor.

Ellen Oh, CEO and cofounder of We Need Diverse Books (https://diversebooks.org), encourages writers to create stories that reflect the diversity of the world we live in. Her advice to those who write about IPOC (indigenous people, people of color) is to tell their story properly or be prepared for criticism. Did I need to tell this story? Yes, it is my story too. I did my best to get it right.

Acknowledgments

I claim to be a perennial. Gina Pell is the architect of the concept. She can be found on Twitter @GinaPell or http://thewhatlist.com. Perennials are ever-blooming, relevant people of all ages who know what's happening in the world, stay current with technology, and have friends of all ages. The fact that I have published a book in my seventh decade has proven to me that life offers us new and exciting opportunities at any age. By maintaining friends of all ages, I gain multiple sources in this world of ours. It is impossible for me to stay current with technology unless I seek out others who do.

I am grateful for family and friends who have encouraged me and confirmed my belief that I needed to tell this story. Maureen Mahon challenged me to write it. Michelle Cameron guided me to find my voice. I have finished my debut novel with her gentle and encouraging mentoring and editing. Elaine Belz and Agnes Golding believed I could do it. Mally Becker, Laura Romain, Niv Miyasato, Connie Fowler, Mary Rahill, Margo Key, Karla Diaz, and Suzanne Moyers, from my Writers Circle writing groups, listened week after week, year after year, and offered insights and advice.

Thanks to my beta readers—Gary Clarke, Evelyn Counts, Judy Pickney, and Roz Miller Choice—who generously gave their time to read early drafts and then provided me with detailed comments, and especially to Susan Follett, whose strong, no-nonsense advice kept me improving the manuscript.

Thanks to Amy Hill Hearth, who guided me to improve the manuscript and encouraged me with specific references to the strong scenes and pinpointed some that needed attention. Her generous support on this journey helped me to believe that this story has value.

Annie Tucker, you are an exceptional editor. You pushed me to improve the manuscript one more time. Your attention to detail is incredible. Katie Caruana polished the manuscript with her proofreading.

Thank you to Brooke Warner, Lauren Wise, Julie Metz, and everyone else at She Writes Press for your innovative vision. Thank you to the whole She Writes community, especially the New York–area group; I am so pleased to be included in this amazing group of women authors.

Thanks to my family: my sister, Celeste, who is my go-to tech support; and my daughters, Elisa, Carla, and Laura, who read my final manuscript on their laptops and gave me the younger generation's perspective. Thanks to my sons-in-law, Brian, Mike, and Philip, who cheered me on, and to my grand-daughters, Mia, Emelia, and Courtney, and grandsons, Max, Kellan, and Jake, who are waiting to read the book that their grandmother wrote. I am hopeful that they will live in a future that doesn't judge people by the color of their skin.

To my husband, Manny, my life partner, the one person who shared the year this story is based on, the one who knows me better than anyone else, you are in my future, my past and my present—I love you forever.

About the Author

Eileen Sanchez is retired after a forty-year career in education. She started as a teacher and ended as a district administrator. She is a reader, a writer, and a perennial—a person with a no-age mindset. Family and friends are the most important parts of her life, followed by traveling and bird watching from her gazebo.

Eileen has been writing for seven years with a writers' group, the Writers Circle, in Summit, New Jersey (www.writerscircleworkshops.com). She is a member of the Historical Writers of America, the Historical Novel Society, the Philadelphia Stories writers' community, Goodreads' American Historical Novels group, and several online writers' groups on LinkedIn and Facebook.

Book Club
Discussion Questions

1. Colleen married a Hispanic man in 1969, when some states still had laws that prohibited or strongly discouraged marriages between individuals of different skin tones or races. Those laws have changed. Why? How?

2. Although the book does not clearly state this, Colleen grew up in a sundown town. What does that term refer to? Do such towns exist today?

3. The characters Jan, Rita, and Beau reflect the views of segregationists. Do you know people with those opinions today? How can we change those views?

4. Colleen was accused of helping black family members register to vote, like church ladies from the North did. What do you know about that effort? Did she have reason to be afraid?

5. Evelyn was proud to be a third-generation, college-educated teacher following her mother, aunts, and grandmother. Did you know about the legacy of black college education before you read this book, or did it surprise you?

6. What other middle-class professions for blacks are represented in the novel? Why do you think the author included them?

7. Why do you think Mr. Peterson assigned Evelyn to mentor Colleen? What did they have in common? What did they learn from each other?

8. During the school year, Colleen was frequently the only white person in a group. Think of a situation in which you were the "only" one in a group. Were you comfortable? Why? Why not?

9. When the segregated schools were combined, the black high school students lost their positions on student council, the football team, and the cheerleading squad. The novel focuses on the seniors who lost other school social opportunities and risked losing the privilege to graduate. Did you expect the student demonstration to remain nonviolent? Why did it?

10. Frank feared that he and his family might be hurt, even killed, as retribution for his revealing his suspicions about his father's death. Did you think his effort to protect his family was courageous, or did he take the easy way out by giving Mr. Peterson the evidence he'd hidden?

11. The midyear overnight closure of the black school and its mandated integration into the white school was enforced through the illegal continued use of a Freedom of Choice plan. *Brown v. Board of Education*, the Supreme Court decision issued in 1954, wasn't fully successful in enforcing school desegregation. Five years after the Civil Rights Act of 1964, it took the threat of financial loss to integrate the schools. Are more laws necessary to enforce integration and civil rights today?

SELECTED TITLES
FROM SHE WRITES PRESS

She Writes Press is an independent publishing company
founded to serve women writers everywhere.
Visit us at www.shewritespress.com.

In a Silent Way by Mary Jo Hetzel. $16.95, 978-1-63152-135-5. When
Jeanna Kendall—a young white teacher at a progressive urban
school—becomes involved with a community activist group, she
finds herself grappling with issues of racism, sexism, and oppression
of various shades in both her professional and personal life.

The Rooms Are Filled by Jessica Null Vealitzek. $16.95, 978-
1-938314-58-2. The coming-of-age story of two outcasts—a
nine-year-old boy who just lost his father, and a closeted young
woman—brought together by circumstance.

Class Letters: Instilling Intangible Lessons through Letters by Claire
Chilton Lopez. $16.95, 978-1-938314-28-5. A high school English
teacher discovers surprising truths about her students when she
exchanges letters with them over the course of a school year.

American Family by Catherine Marshall-Smith. $16.95, 978-
1631521638. Partners Richard and Michael, recovering alcohol-
ics, struggle to gain custody of Richard's biological daughter from
her grandparents after her mother's death only to discover they—
and she—are fundamentalist Christians.

Shelter Us by Laura Diamond. $16.95, 978-1-63152-970-2. Lawyer-
turned-stay-at-home-mom Sarah Shaw is still struggling to find
a steady happiness after the death of her infant daughter when
she meets a young homeless mother and toddler she can't get out
of her mind—and becomes determined to rescue them.

Again and Again by Ellen Bravo. $16.95, 978-1-63152-939-9.
When the man who raped her roommate in college becomes a
Senate candidate, women's rights leader Deborah Borenstein
must make a choice—one that could determine control of the Senate, the course of a friendship, and the fate of a marriage.